A Fine How Do You Do

Clint carried his coffee over to the table where the girl was sitting. She was looking around, seemingly unconcerned about sitting in a saloon crowded with half-drunk men. Abruptly, she looked up at him and followed his progress until he reached her.

Lem hadn't asked her name, so Clint simply said, "I hear you're looking for me."

"I was told you would not be finished playing poker for some time," she said.

"I'm not finished," he said. "We're on a break."

"So you are Mr. Adams?"

"That's right."

"Please," she said, "I want to be very clear. You are the Gunsmith?"

"I am."

That was when she took a gun out of her purse and shot him.

DON'T MISS THESE
ALL-ACTION WESTERN SERIES
FROM THE BERKLEY PUBLISHING GROUP

THE GUNSMITH by J. R. Roberts

Clint Adams was a legend among lawmen, outlaws, and ladies. They called him . . . the Gunsmith.

LONGARM by Tabor Evans

The popular long-running series about Deputy U.S. Marshal Custis Long—his life, his loves, his fight for justice.

SLOCUM by Jake Logan

Today's longest-running action Western. John Slocum rides a deadly trail of hot blood and cold steel.

BUSHWHACKERS by B. J. Lanagan

An action-packed series by the creators of Longarm! The rousing adventures of the most brutal gang of cutthroats ever assembled—Quantrill's Raiders.

DIAMONDBACK by Guy Brewer

Dex Yancey is Diamondback, a Southern gentleman turned con man when his brother cheats him out of the family fortune. Ladies love him. Gamblers hate him. But nobody pulls one over on Dex . . .

WILDGUN by Jack Hanson

The blazing adventures of mountain man Will Barlow—from the creators of Longarm!

TEXAS TRACKER by Tom Calhoun

J.T. Law: the most relentless—and dangerous—manhunter in all Texas. Where sheriffs and posses fail, he's the best man to bring in the most vicious outlaws—for a price.

THE GUNSMITH

357

THE DEAD RINGER

J. R. ROBERTS

J

JOVE BOOKS, NEW YORK

THE BERKLEY PUBLISHING GROUP
Published by the Penguin Group
Penguin Group (USA) Inc.
375 Hudson Street, New York, New York 10014, USA

Penguin Group (Canada), 90 Eglinton Avenue East, Suite 700, Toronto, Ontario M4P 2Y3, Canada
(a division of Pearson Penguin Canada Inc.)
Penguin Books Ltd., 80 Strand, London WC2R 0RL, England
Penguin Group Ireland, 25 St. Stephen's Green, Dublin 2, Ireland (a division of Penguin Books Ltd.)
Penguin Group (Australia), 250 Camberwell Road, Camberwell, Victoria 3124, Australia
(a division of Pearson Australia Group Pty. Ltd.)
Penguin Books India Pvt. Ltd., 11 Community Centre, Panchsheel Park, New Delhi—110 017, India
Penguin Group (NZ), 67 Apollo Drive, Rosedale, Auckland 0632, New Zealand
(a division of Pearson New Zealand Ltd.)
Penguin Books (South Africa) (Pty.) Ltd., 24 Sturdee Avenue, Rosebank, Johannesburg 2196,
South Africa

Penguin Books Ltd., Registered Offices: 80 Strand, London WC2R 0RL, England

This is a work of fiction. Names, characters, places, and incidents either are the product of the author's imagination or are used fictitiously, and any resemblance to actual persons, living or dead, business establishments, events, or locales is entirely coincidental

THE DEAD RINGER

A Jove Book / published by arrangement with the author

PRINTING HISTORY
Jove edition / September 2011

Copyright © 2011 by Robert J. Randisi.
Cover illustration by Sergio Giovine.

ISBN: 978-0-515-14991-3

JOVE®
Jove Books are published by The Berkley Publishing Group,
a division of Penguin Group (USA) Inc.,
375 Hudson Street, New York, New York 10014.
JOVE® is a registered trademark of Penguin Group (USA) Inc.
The "J" design is a trademark of Penguin Group (USA) Inc.

PRINTED IN THE UNITED STATES OF AMERICA

10 9 8 7 6 5 4 3 2 1

ONE

Clint was in Tucson to play poker.

Not in the saloons, even though there were plenty of games there. Those games were for small change, and Clint played in such games only to kill time. No, he was in Tucson to play in a private game, which was being held in a back room of the Green Garter Saloon.

A curtained doorway led to the room, and there were two armed guards on the inside, to make sure no one interrupted the game—to rob it, or for any other reason.

Clint had secured the chair with his back to the wall, from which he would be able to see anyone coming through that doorway.

There were four other men at the table, none of whom Clint had ever played with before. It was one of the reasons he had accepted the invitation. He had been in many games with the likes of Bat Masterson and Luke Short—good friends and worthy foes at the table—but he enjoyed playing with men he'd never met before. It gave him an opportunity to read new people, figure out their tells, and hone his own talents.

The curtain parted and a saloon girl entered carrying a tray of drinks. The other players had all ordered drinks—beer and whiskey—but Clint had not. He did not drink while he played poker.

The girl set the drinks down at the elbows of the men, only one of whom bothered to thank and tip her. His name was Grant Sutherland and, as far as Clint could see during this first three hours of the game, was probably his chief competitor.

Sutherland appeared to be in his late thirties, was the only player who actually dressed like a gambler—boiled white shirt, string tie, and black suit. He had manners, his suit was expensive, and he was drinking brandy. And the girls liked him, because he was handsome.

It seemed to Clint that Grant Sutherland pretty much had it all. He handled the cards well, too. He could have cheated if Clint hadn't been sitting there. He doubted the other players would have been able to tell.

The invitation had come from the owner of the Green Garter, Andy McLintock, whom Clint had known for over ten years. For all that time McLintock had owned one saloon or another, in different towns. So when the telegram had come from Tucson, Clint had not been surprised. He'd accepted the invitation readily, especially when Andy told him there would not be any of the usual players.

The saloon girl finished setting her drinks down and left the room. The guards made sure the curtains were closed so no one could peer in.

The house dealer said, "Comin' out, gents," and dealt the next hand.

As the saloon girl came out of the back room, the batwing doors opened and another woman entered the saloon. Actually, she was a girl and, although pretty, did not attract attention for that reason. It was simply the fact that a girl had entered the saloon. Not only that, but she headed straight for the bar.

The bartender watched in disbelief as the girl approached him. The men at the bar actually parted to give her room, but they stared as she spoke to the bartender.

"Excuse me?" she said.

"Miss," the barman said, "you shouldn't be in here."

"I'm looking for someone," she said. "I was told at his hotel that he might be here."

The bartender, a man in his fifties, adopted the look of an impatient father as he asked, "Who you lookin' for?"

"Clint Adams," she said.

Nobody said anything. She looked around, as if she had just become aware that she was the center of attention.

"Is there a problem?" she asked the bartender. "Is he not here?"

"Oh, he's here," the bartender said. "He's in the back room."

"Oh, wonderful," she said. "Can you just point me in the direction—"

"You can't go back there, miss."

"Why not?"

"There's a poker game goin' on."

"Oh." She looked around again, then back at the bartender. "Well, how long will he be playing?"

"There's no way of knowin' that, miss," the bartender said.

"I see," she said. "Well . . . I suppose I'll just have to wait for him to be finished."

"Here?" the bartender asked.

"Well, yes," she said. "If I could just have a table, and a drink?"

The bartender looked around. There were no empty tables, but the girl seemed determined to wait. He looked at one of the men standing at the bar, staring at the girl.

"Eddie," he said. "Get the lady a table, will ya?"

"Sure, Lem."

Eddie Bricker, a hand at one of the nearby ranches, said, "Miss? This way."

"Thank you," she said. "And my drink?" she said to the bartender.

"Sure, what'll ya have, miss?"

"A glass of whiskey, please."

"Whiskey?" Lem asked. "Are you sure?"

"Quite sure, thank you. Sir?" she said to Eddie.

"Yes, miss," Eddie said. He spotted a table where two of his friends were sitting. He was sure he could get them to move and make room for the young woman.

"Just follow me, miss."

"I'll have your drink brought over," Lem said.

"Thank you both," she said. "You're very kind."

TWO

The game sorted itself out very quickly.

"Quickly" is a relative term, however.

Some of these private games had been known to go on for days. Clint was starting to understand why the usual suspects weren't there, and why he had been invited.

These players had money, but they just weren't very good. While it was true that Bat Masterson, Luke Short, Brady Hawkes, Bret and Bart Maverick, Henry Deringer, and others played poker to make money, they also played for the competition. If they knew there was none at a game, they didn't show up.

Clint now knew he had been invited because those professionals had turned the invite down.

The only two players with extensive knowledge of the game were Clint and Sutherland. The others, while they had money, quickly fell by the wayside, and after six hours the game came down to him and Grant Sutherland.

As the last of the other players put on his jacket and left the room, the dealer said, "Time for a break, gents."

The dealer, a man with good hands who had been doing it for twenty years, stood and cracked his knuckles.

"Half an hour," he said, and left the room. The guards remained, and would stay as long as there were chips on the table.

Sutherland stood up and looked at Clint.

"Drink?" he asked.

"Coffee," Clint said.

"Your choice."

They walked past the guards and through the curtains, secure that their money would be safe. They walked through the crowded saloon to the bar, where they knew they could have anything they wanted for free.

"Beer," Sutherland told the bartender, Lem.

"Coffee," Clint said.

The bartender brought Sutherland's beer, set Clint's coffee before him, and said, "Mr. Adams, there's somebody here lookin' for you."

"Oh?" Clint sipped his coffee. "Who's that?"

"A young lady," Lem said. "She came in and asked if you was here. I told her you was, but that you were playing poker. I said she could see you until you was done."

"That's fine," Clint said. "Where'd she go?"

"Nowhere," Lem said. "She's here."

"Here?" Clint asked, surprised. He looked around. "Where?"

"She's sittin' at a table over against that wall," Lem said. "Drinkin' whiskey."

Clint craned his neck to have a look.

"Her? She looks like a kid."

"Yeah, she does," Lem said, "but that kid is workin' on her second glass of whiskey."

"Whiskey?"

Lem nodded and said, "The good stuff."

Sutherland took a look at the girl.

"Is she willin' to wait until the card game is over?" he asked.

"She says she's gonna sit there and wait, yeah," Lem said.

"Anybody bothering her?" Clint asked.

"Not since she said she was here to see you," Lem said. "Said she went to your hotel and they sent her over here."

"Did she say what she wanted?"

"No," Lem said, "just that she wanted to talk to you."

"Well," Clint said, "since we're on a break, maybe I better find out what she wants, before she does get herself in trouble."

"I'd appreciate that, Mr. Adams," Lem said. "The last thing Mr. McLintock wants in his place is trouble with some girl."

"Warm that up for me, will you?" Clint asked, putting his mug on the bar so the bartender could refill it. "Then I'll go over and see what she wants."

Clint carried his coffee over to the table where the girl was sitting. She was looking around, seemingly unconcerned about sitting in a saloon crowded with half-drunk men. Abruptly, she looked up at him and followed his progress until he reached her.

Lem hadn't asked her name, so Clint simply said, "I hear you're looking for me."

"I was told you would not be finished playing poker for some time," she said.

"I'm not finished," he said. "We're on a break."

"So you are Mr. Adams?"

"That's right."

"Please," she said, "I want to be very clear. You are the Gunsmith?"

"I am."

That was when she took a gun out of her purse and shot him.

THREE

It was a two-shot derringer, and she fired only one. The bullet hit him in the left shoulder, felt like a bee sting. The saloon was so noisy that no one but the men at a nearby table heard the shot. One of them leaped to his feet and grabbed the gun from her before she could trigger the second barrel.

"Hey, mister," he asked, "you all right?"

Clint looked down, saw some blood on his left shoulder, but the pain still wasn't very bad.

"I think I'm okay," he said. He still had his coffee cup in his right hand, so he set it down and then used his fingers to probe the wound. "Yeah, I'm okay."

"You oughta see the doc," the man said, still holding the derringer.

Clint looked at the girl. She was staring straight ahead, not paying any attention to what was going on around her.

"I guess we oughta take her over to the sheriff's office," the other man said. "You know where the doc's office is?"

"No," Clint said.

"Neil, take this fella to the doc's," the man said to one of his friends. "I'll take the girl to the sheriff's office." He looked at Clint again. "You can come over there when you get patched up."

"Yeah, sure," Clint said. "Wait. Who are you?"

"My name's Doug Bradford," the man said. He moved aside his vest to show a badge on his chest. "Deputy."

The deputy took the girl by the arm and pulled her to her feet.

"Miss, you're under arrest."

Clint told Grant Sutherland what had happened, and where he was going.

"Sure, I understand," Sutherland said, frowning at the spread of blood on Clint's shirt. "You sure you're okay?"

"I'll be fine," Clint said, "as soon as the doctor patches me up."

"You sure you're gonna be able to play?"

"Don't worry," Clint said. "I'll play. You let Andy know, okay?"

"Sure, sure," Sutherland said. "I'll see you later."

Clint nodded and went with the man called Neil to the doctor's office.

The doctor's name was Foster. He was a healthy-looking sixty, had been the doctor in Tucson for twelve years, since coming out West.

He got Clint's shirt off and probed the wound.

"It's a small bullet," he said, "not much damage. I guess you ought to be grateful she was a bad shot, even from up close."

"A bad shot? She very calmly pulled the trigger and hit me, Doc."

"She could've hit you in the heart," the sawbones said. "Or the eye. This won't even keep you off your feet for an hour."

"It's not my feet I'm worried about, Doc," Clint said. "I've got to be able to play poker."

"I don't see a problem with that," Doc Foster said. "I'll get the bullet out and patch you up." He laughed.

"What's funny?"

"I'll probably do more damage probing for the bullet than the bullet itself did."

"Maybe we should just leave it in there," Clint suggested.

The doctor laughed again and said, "Don't worry, Mr. Adams. I'm sure you've been through this many times before."

FOUR

When Clint got to the sheriff's office, the deputy, Bradford, was sitting behind the desk. There was no one else in sight.

"Is the sheriff out?" he asked.

"He's out, all right," Bradford said. "Out of town. I've got the girl in a cell. What'd Doc say?"

"It's not bad," Clint said. "Won't keep me from doing anything I want to do."

"What do you want to do?"

"Right now, I want to talk to the girl and find out why she shot me."

"You're Adams, right? Involved in that private poker game?"

"That's right."

"Guess you coulda shot her before she shot you."

"Guess I could have, if I'd seen it coming," Clint said. "She caught me flat-footed."

"Coulda killed you."

"With that little gun, she would've had to hit me in the heart," he said, "or the eye."

"She say anything before she shot you?"

"Just asked me my name."

"Sure you wanna go in?"

"Did you search her?"

"Yep," Bradford said. "She don't have another gun on her."

"Then I'll go in."

"Suit yerself," Bradford said. "Want the keys?"

"No," Clint said, "I'll talk to her through the bars. Want me to leave my gun here?"

"You gonna shoot her?"

"No."

Bradford waved at him to go ahead.

Clint went into the cell block, which was empty but for the girl. The other cell doors were wide open.

She was sitting on her cot, so Clint entered the cell next to hers and sat on the cot there. That put him right next to her, with only the bars between them.

"What's your name?" he asked.

"Isobel."

"Why'd you shoot me, Isobel?" he asked.

"Because of what you did to my brother."

"Your brother?" he asked. "Who's your brother?"

"Andrew Escalante."

"Escalante?" he asked. "Mexican?"

"Our father is Mexican," she said. "Our mother was American. She died several years ago."

"And what did I do to your brother, Andrew—who I've never met, by the way."

She turned her head to look at him, her black eyes flashing.

"So you say!" she snapped. "He says different."

"So he's still alive?"

"No thanks to you!"

"But where is he?"

"He is in prison," she said.

"For what?"

"For a murder you committed."

"And where was I supposed to have committed this murder?"

"South of here," she said. "Just outside a town called Tubac."

"Tubac," he said. "I've never been to Tubac."

"I said outside of Tubac."

"Well, then, I've never even been outside of Tubac," he said. "Is that where your brother is in jail?"

"Yes."

"And who said I committed a murder?"

"He told me himself."

"That he was innocent and I was guilty?"

"Yes."

"When is this murder supposed to have happened, Isobel?"

"Four days ago."

"I got here, to Tucson, only three days ago."

"So? You could have come here directly from Tubac."

"I've never been in—or near—Tubac."

"That's what you say!"

He figured he had to try something else.

"Okay, who am I supposed to have murdered?"

"A man named Joe Widmar."

He frowned. He didn't know a man named Widmar. Had never heard of him. But he knew what Isobel would say to that.

"Has your brother stood trial yet?"

"No," she said. "Not yet."

"So instead of waiting to see if he would be found guilty, you decided to come here and kill me?"

"He will be found guilty."

"Why do you say that?"

"He is Mexican."

Clint stood up.

"Okay," he said.

She stared at him.

"I'll talk to you later."

"About what?" she asked. "Now I am in jail, too, and I will be tried for attempted murder. I am only sorry I did not kill you."

"You didn't try very hard, Isobel," he said. "I just don't think it's in you."

"It is not in my brother either."

"We'll see."

He walked out of the cell. Before he could leave the cell block, she got up and ran to the bars, gripping them tightly.

"What do you mean, 'We'll see'?" she asked.

He turned and looked at her.

"I mean you and me will head for Tubac tomorrow to straighten this out."

"You and me?"

"Yes."

"Then . . . I will not be kept in jail?"

"You will tonight," he said. "But tomorrow you'll be out."

"But . . . why?"

"Because somehow your brother—a man I've never met—is convinced that I killed another man I've never met," he said. "That's something I want to get to the bottom of."

"But, but . . ." she stammered as he turned to leave.

"But what?"

"Can't you let me out now?"

He grinned at her.

"No, you're going to spend the rest of the night in jail," he said. "Maybe you'll think twice the next time you want to shoot somebody."

FIVE

When Clint came out of the cell blocks, the deputy looked up from the desk.

"So?"

"I'm going to want her released tomorrow morning," he said.

"What?"

"I'm not pressing charges," Clint added, "but I want you to hold her overnight."

"What's goin' on?" Bradford asked. "She tried to kill you."

"Not really," Clint said. "From that range, if she wanted to kill me, I think she would have."

"But why release her?"

"I'm going to take her to her brother."

"Where's her brother?"

"A town called Tubac."

"That's south of here some," Bradford said. "Almost to Nogales."

Clint knew there were two cities called Nogales, one in the United States and one in Mexico.

"What's goin' on?" Bradford asked.

Clint explained the girl's reason for shooting him.

"So you're gonna go to Tubac to find out who really did kill this fella, what's 'is name?"

"Widmar," Clint said. "That name mean anything to you?"

"Not a thing."

"What do you know about Tubac?"

"Small town, close to Mexico but they don't like Mexicans there."

"Why not?"

Bradford shrugged. "Why does anybody dislike Mexicans?"

"Well," Clint said, "I guess I'm going to be spending a few days in Tubac."

"What about your poker game?" Bradford asked.

"I'll have to try to finish it tonight," Clint said. "There are only two of us left."

"What if you don't finish?"

"Guess I'll have to decide what's more important," Clint said, "a boy's life, or a poker game."

Clint returned to the saloon, asked the bartender for a beer. He carried it to the back room, where he found three men—Sutherland, the dealer, and Andy McLintock—sitting at the table.

"Hey!" McLintock said, getting to his feet. "I heard about the shooting. How are you?"

"I'm okay," Clint said, sitting down. All he had was a bit

of an ache in his shoulder. "Luckily, it was a small-caliber bullet, and her heart really wasn't in killing me."

"So, you're okay to play?" Andy asked.

"For a while."

"What's that mean?" Sutherland asked.

"I've got to go to Tubac tomorrow," Clint explained, "so we're going to have to finish this off tonight."

"And if we don't?" Andy asked.

"I'll have to withdraw tomorrow," Clint said. "Sutherland will win."

"I don't wanna win that way," Sutherland said. "Let's sit down and play and see what happens. If we're not finished by mornin' so you can leave, we'll just play a one-hand showdown for all of it."

"You'd be willin' to do that?" McLintock asked.

"Why not?" Sutherland asked. "I'd rather win it or lose it that way than by a forfeit."

"Well," Clint said, "let's get started then, and we'll see what happens."

SIX

Andrew Escalante looked out the barred window of his cell to the people walking by on the Tubac streets.

"Get away from the window, Mex," the deputy shouted from behind him.

Andrew turned and looked across the room. There was only one cell in the Tubac sheriff's office, and it was in plain sight of the sheriff's desk. At the moment, the sheriff wasn't sitting at his desk; Deputy Hank Deeds was. Deeds didn't like Mexicans, and relished having one in the cell.

"Ain't nobody comin' ta help you, Mex," Deeds said, laughing, "so you might as well stop lookin' out the window."

Andrew stepped away from the window and sat down on his hard cot. His sister, Isobel, had promised to help him, but he hadn't seen her in a couple of days. He didn't know what she could do for him anyway. Maybe plead with their father to help him, but Don Alfredo had not wanted his two children to cross the border from Mexico into the United States. When they were determined to do so despite his objection, he told them they would be on their own.

Andrew put his head in his hands. He didn't know why he had listened to what Clint Adams had told him. He had been impressed to meet the famous Gunsmith, but Adams had turned out to be something other than the man Andrew thought he was.

And now he was in jail for murder.

Jack Hendricks had been the sheriff of Tubac for three years. For the most part, the town fathers let him do his job his way, but every so often they called him in and gave him some sort of instruction. As long as he followed those instructions, he kept his job.

Today was such a day.

He entered the City Hall and presented himself to the Town Council.

"Thanks for comin' so quickly, Sheriff," Mayor Victor Stoffer said.

The summons had come only fifteen minutes ago, and he knew better than to keep them waiting.

Also in the room with the mayor were the four other members of the Council, all merchants in town, and one lawyer. But the mayor was the spokesman, and they all deferred to him.

"Sure, Mayor."

"How's young Escalante doin' in his cell?" the mayor asked.

"He ain't happy, Mayor," Hendricks said.

"Well, that's too bad," the mayor said. "You feedin' him?"

"Yessir."

"Good, good," Stoffer said. "He talk to you about the murder?"

"No," Hendricks said, "he's keeping quiet about it."

"Well, if he keeps quiet, he's gonna hang," Mayor Stoffer said. "Does he know that?"

"He knows."

"Then why's he keepin' quiet?"

Hendricks shrugged and said, "Maybe he's hopin' his sister or his father will come and save him."

"Well, we know the old man ain't gonna come to help him," Stoffer said. "Where's the sister?"

"Don't know," Hendricks said. "She left town a couple of days ago and ain't come back yet."

"You think she went for help?" Stoffer asked. "Maybe gonna come back with some guns?"

"She's just a girl, Mayor," Hendricks said. "I don't think she's out recruiting gunmen to come and break her brother out of jail."

"Good, good," Stoffer said. "Well, keep workin' on the lad. Get him to talk. Remind him he's gonna hang."

"Yes, sir."

"Get us the information we need, Sheriff," Stoffer said, "and we won't forget it."

"Yessir."

"That's all."

Sheriff Hendricks nodded and backed out of the room.

Stoffer looked up and down the Council table at the other members and asked, "What do you think?"

They all started talking at once.

In Mexico, about twenty miles south of Nogales, Don Alfredo Escalante was staring out a window of his own; only what he saw was not a Tubac street. He was staring out the window of his hacienda, and all he saw were the walls that surrounded it, and some of his vaqueros working with horses in the corral.

He wanted his son to be out there working with them, but he had chosen to go across the border to seek his own fortune. And as if that was not bad enough, he had taken his little sister with him.

A proud man, Don Alfredo did not appreciate his children leaving him, so he had told them they would be on their own if anything happened.

And it had.

He had received word from Tubac that his son was in jail, charged with murdering a gringo. His first instinct was to take some of his vaqueros to Tubac to retrieve his son, but he stopped himself. He had told them they would be on their own, and he'd meant it.

He heard his wife come into the room behind him. If he was disappointed in his children, she was disappointed in her husband. She wanted her stepson back, whom she loved as her own child, but Don Alfredo refused to go and get him.

"My husband—"

"Do not plead with me again, Doña Estrella," he said. "My mind is made up."

"I simply wished to tell you that lunch is ready, my husband," she said quietly.

"Very well," he said. "I will be there."

She left the room without further word. He watched his vaqueros for several more seconds, then turned and followed her.

SEVEN

Clint didn't think he'd have time to spend with Teresa Solano before he left for Tubac, but the poker gods had smiled on him only a couple of hours into the continuation of the game. Grant Sutherland's luck had abandoned him, and rather than having to play a one-hand showdown, Clint had managed to clean Sutherland out in three hours—the last hour being the key.

Theresa was waiting for him in his room when he got there, naked in bed.

"This is where I left you this morning," he said, smiling.

"Well," she said, rubbing her hands over the brown nipples that topped her small but firm breasts, "I got up after you left, got dressed, went down for breakfast, then worked at the café and came back up here to wait for you."

"You sure you just didn't stay here all day?" he asked.

"I'm sure," she said, sliding her hands down between her legs.

She was a tall, dark-haired Mexican waitress he'd met at

a café down the street. She'd gone back to his hotel room with him the first night and demonstrated an amazing appetite for sex. After that she'd spent the night with him, and then the next two.

It was only 4 a.m. when he got to his room, so there was still time for part of another night together before he left town.

But he didn't tell her he'd be leaving in the morning. He didn't want to upset her. So he simply undressed and got into bed with her. Her nipples were already hard, and her pussy very wet, and she was on him eagerly, pushing him down on his back and mounting him, taking his already hard cock into her wet, steamy depths.

"*Ayyy*," she said as she settled down on him and took the length of him inside. She started to ride him up and down, wetting him thoroughly with her juices, and then she let him slide free, shimmied down between his legs, and took him into her mouth. She sucked him avidly, kneading his balls with one hand while she stroked him with the other, all the while sliding him in and out of her mouth.

She worked him to the point of bursting before he pushed her off him, flipped her onto her back, and returned the favor. Her pussy juices wet his cheeks and forehead as he licked and nibbled her into a frenzy, and then as she trembled and writhed beneath him, he mounted her and slammed his cock into her. He fucked her hard, the way she liked it, and was able to hold back so that they went on that way for some time. He bit his lip and fought for control, but just as she arched her back beneath him and screamed into the pillow, he also exploded, bellowing like a bull with no pillow to mask the sound . . .

* * *

That first morning when he had come down to the lobby, he'd received a knowing look from the desk clerk. That was how he knew that they could be heard all the way down there while they had sex. After he told Teresa, she began to bury her face in the pillow to muffle her screams. He, however, was not as shy, so usually two or three times a night he would end up shouting or grunting loud enough to be heard. This night was no different, and he ended up lying next to her, his throat sore while he continued to stroke her pussy with his left hand. She closed her thighs on his hand and writhed as he inserted two fingers into her, and her spasms went on for some time that way . . .

He had become very familiar with the female orgasm over the years, but he had never met a woman whose pleasure went on as long as Teresa's. And as a result of that, the sheets beneath her usually ended up soaked with her juices, and to sleep they'd have to huddle together on the other side of the bed. Then during the night, for more sex, they'd just move back to the wet side, and wet it some more. By morning the room was filled with the smells of their couplings.

On this morning he woke early enough to wash himself with the pitcher and basin on the dresser.

"So early?" she moaned from the bed.

"I have to leave town," he said.

"What?"

"Just for a few days."

That woke her up. She propped herself up on her elbows.

"Why did you not tell me?" she asked. "We could have made the night memorable."

"Teresa," he said to her, "every night with you has been memorable."

"Then you will be coming back?" she asked hopefully.

"Oh yes," he said, strapping on his gun, "I'll be back this way soon."

"When?"

"Soon," he said again. He went to the bed and kissed her. "I'll only be spending a few days in Tubac."

EIGHT

Clint entered the sheriff's office, and Deputy Bradford turned to face him, holding a mug of coffee.

"Mornin'," he said. "Come for the girl?"

"Yep."

"Still not gonna press charges?"

"Nope."

Bradford shrugged, put his mug down.

"I'll get 'er."

He went into the cell block, came out with a rumpled-looking Isobel Escalante.

"You *pendejo*!" she spat at Clint. "You made me spend all night in jail."

"You did that to yerself, miss," the deputy said, "by shootin' this man."

"Do you want to yell at me," Clint asked her, "or do you want to get some breakfast before we head for Tubac?"

"Breakfast," she said. "And perhaps someplace where I can clean up?"

Clint looked at Bradford.

"I got a pitcher and basin in the back," the deputy said. "I'll get you some water."

Isobel looked only slightly better when she and Clint entered the café. They sat down and Clint ordered a pot of coffee.

"*Huevos rancheros*," Isobel said to the waitress.

"Steak and eggs," Clint said.

"Comin' up," the middle-aged woman said. She started walking away, then stopped and looked at Clint. "You know if Teresa's comin' to work today?"

"I think she'll be here."

"If she ain't, she's fired," the woman said, and went off to the kitchen.

"Your girlfriend?" Isobel asked.

"No, just a friend."

The woman came back with a pot of coffee and two mugs, filled them both, and left. Isobel attacked the coffee and then poured some more.

"That was very mean, what you did to me," she said.

"Isobel," he said, "you shot me."

"You deserved it for what you did to my brother."

"I told you," he said, "I never met your brother. I've never been to Tubac."

"Why are you lying?"

"Somebody's lying," he said. "Maybe it's your brother."

"No," she said, "he would not lie to me."

"Then somebody lied to him," Clint said. "Did you ever think of that?"

She stared at him.

"You mean someone pretended to be you?" she asked.

"Could be."

"Why would someone do that?"

"I don't know," Clint said, "but we'll find out something when we get to Tubac. We'll go and see your brother and find out if he's ever met me."

"And if he has?"

"Don't worry," Clint said, "he hasn't. Unless . . ."

"Unless what?"

"Unless he met me while he was using another name," Clint said. "What's Andrew look like?"

"He is very handsome," she said.

"That doesn't help."

The waitress came with their plates and set them down. Isobel immediately attacked her food, and Clint decided to suspend the conversation while they ate.

"Do you have a horse?" Clint asked after breakfast.

"No."

"How did you get here, then?"

"Well, yes, I do have a horse," she said, "but I came in a buggy."

"And where is it now?"

"At the livery stable."

"Good," he said, "That's where my horse is, too. Let's go."

He saddled Eclipse first, then hitched Isobel's horse to her buggy and walked it outside.

"You know the way to Tubac," he said, helping her into the seat. "I'll follow you."

"And if I try to get away?"

"Why would you?" he asked. "We're going there to help your brother."

"Or to kill him?"

"Why would I kill him?"

"So he can't tell what really happened."

"Why would I leave him alive, come here," Clint asked, "and then go back to kill him? If he and I were together in Tubac, why wouldn't I have just killed him then?"

She stared at him, then said, "I don't know."

"Then let's go to Tubac and find out."

NINE

Tubac was about thirty miles south of Tucson. Clint could have made it easily if he had been alone, but Isobel's buggy was slowing them down.

When they had to stop the third time for her, Clint started to doubt they'd make it to Tubac before dark. It hadn't occurred to him when they left, so they didn't have any supplies.

"I'm sorry," she said. "I'm tired. The night in jail—I didn't sleep very well."

"I understand," he said. "We'll go slower."

"We won't get there tonight, then," she said.

"Maybe not," he said. "We can camp on the trail."

"We have no supplies."

"We have water," he said. "I have a coffeepot and coffee, and some beef jerky."

"You could get there if you left me behind."

"That's not an option."

"I will get there as fast as I can."

"No."

"Why not?"

"I'm not going to leave you alone out here."

"That is . . . very gallant," she said, giving him a puzzled look. "Considering I shot you."

"Look," he said, "it's not imperative that we get there tonight. We can find out what we need to tomorrow, just as well."

"I can go further," she said. "We can travel until dark."

"Okay," he said, "but then we'll stop and camp."

"As you say, *Señor* Adams."

"Clint," he said. "Just call me Clint."

"Are you always this . . . nice to people who shoot you?" she asked.

"No," he said, "just pretty women who shoot me."

"How many of those have there been?"

"Too many," he said.

They traveled until dark, and then Clint unhitched her horse, unsaddled Eclipse, and built a fire. He had the coffeepot going in no time. He handed Isobel a cup of coffee and a piece of dry beef jerky.

"You are . . . a strange man," she said.

"No, I'm not."

"Well, to me you are. Any other man would have shot me yesterday."

"Is that what you wanted?"

"What?"

"You shot me because you wanted me to kill you?"

"N-No, not at all."

"Then why didn't you shoot me in the heart?"

"I . . . rushed the shot," she said.

"Are you normally a good shot with that belly gun?"

"Belly gun?"

"The derringer."

"I can usually shoot what I aim at."

"Well, you hit me," he said. "Have you ever killed anyone?"

"Is that important?"

"You haven't, have you."

"No." She sounded like she was apologizing.

"That's nothing to be ashamed of," he said. "Not everybody kills in their lifetime."

"I suppose not."

"What about your brother?" he asked. "Has he ever killed anyone?"

"No," she said. "He has not even killed an animal. My father . . ."

"What about your father?"

"He . . . is ashamed of Andrew," she said. "My father has always been . . . a man of violence. Andrew is . . . gentle."

"Not the son your father wanted, eh?"

"No."

"And what about your mother?"

"As I told you, she died several years ago," Isobel said. "It affected my father . . . terribly. He has remarried, but I do not think he has recovered from my mother's death."

"So he's been harder on your brother since then?"

"My brother, and me. It's why we left."

"What did he do when you did that?"

"He disowned us," she said. "Told us we were on our own."

"So he won't help your brother with this?"

"No."

"Isobel, I don't think you came to me to kill me."

"Then why—"

"I think you wanted my help."

"But you are the cause . . . I mean, I thought you were the cause of it all."

"Maybe you're not sure about Andrew," Clint said, "about his version of what happened."

"So . . . I came to you?"

He shrugged.

"Could be. Look at the result. I'm going to Tubac with you."

"To kill Andrew," she said, "or to help him."

"I know which one is true," he said.

"And I will find out when we get there."

"You better finish eating, and then get some rest," he said. "Do you have any idea how far we are from Tubac right now?"

"Several miles, I think," she said. "Maybe more."

"We'll make it early tomorrow, then," he said. "We won't have to push your horse."

"She's old."

"I know," he said. "This is probably her last hurrah."

"Hurrah?"

He smiled.

"She'll have to be put to pasture when we get to Tubac."

"Yes," she said. "Yes."

"Go ahead," he said. "Go to sleep."

"And you?"

"I'll be up for a while, but don't worry. I'll get some sleep."

"Very well," she said, standing. "Good night . . . Clint."

TEN

Clint awoke first the next morning and made a fresh pot of coffee. When Isobel woke up, he handed her a cup.

"I need a bath," she complained.

"You can have one when we get to Tubac," he said. "It'll make you feel a lot better."

"I want to see Andrew first," she said, "to make sure he is all right."

"Okay," Clint said, "we can do that. We'll get the easy part over with."

"The easy part?"

"Having your brother tell you he's never seen me before."

"I hope that is true," she said.

"Oh, you're starting to like me, huh?"

"No," she said, "if he doesn't know you, it means you can help us."

"I'll help," he said. "You want some jerky for breakfast?"

She made a face.

"Okay," he said, "after we see your brother, we'll get something to eat, and then you can have your bath."

He saddled Eclipse and then hitched up her old mare. The poor horse probably only had a few miles left in her. He only hoped she wouldn't collapse before they got there.

Tubac was small, but busy. There were people on both sides of the main street, all the businesses were open, and there were horses and buckboards on the street.

"The sheriff's office is right there," Isobel said as they rode down the street. Clint looked where she was pointing.

"Okay," he said.

They pulled up in front of the office. Her mare was laboring. Clint was afraid she wasn't going to have to be put out to pasture; she was going to have to be put down.

He helped Isobel down, and they approached the front door.

"What's the sheriff's name?" he asked before they went in.

"Hendricks."

"How long has he had the job?"

"I do not know," she said. "We only met him when we got to town."

"And when was that?"

"Two weeks ago."

"Okay," he said. "Let me do the talking."

"Of course."

They went inside.

Andrew Escalante saw his sister enter the sheriff's office with another man and immediately got to his feet.

"Isobel—"

"Quiet!" Deputy Deeds shouted.

"Shut up, Deeds," Sheriff Hendricks said. "Miss Escalante. I was wondering what happened to you."

Andrew fell silent, wondering who his sister had brought with her, and if the man was going to help him.

Clint saw the single cell with the man in it, assumed this was Andrew. When he called out his sister's name, then he knew.

The deputy was standing by the desk and the sheriff was seated at it.

"Sheriff Hendricks," Isobel said. "I have brought with me a man who may be able to help my brother."

"Only way he's gonna help your brother is if he breaks him out of jail," Deeds said, laughing. He was a mean-looking man about ten years younger than the sheriff, who looked bored. Clint figured the sheriff had been a lawman for a lot of years.

"Goddamnit, Deeds," Hendricks said. "Go and do your rounds."

"I just did 'em—"

"Do them again!"

Deeds looked like he was going to argue, but then he stormed past Clint and Isobel out of the office.

"Who are you?" Hendricks asked Clint.

Clint leaned over the desk and said, "Sheriff, my name's Clint Adams." He was sure the young man in the cell hadn't heard him say his name.

Hendricks looked surprised, then looked over at Andrew in his cell.

"Are you aware that he's been sayin'—"

"I think I know what he's been saying," Clint said. "I came to Tubac to clear things up."

"How do you plan to do that?" the sheriff asked.

"Well, for one thing," Clint said, "I never saw him before, and I'd like for him to say the same thing about me."

"But he's been sayin' you and him were partners, and that you killed the man he's supposed to have killed."

"I know, I know," Clint said. "Can I talk to him?"

"With me listenin', yeah."

"That's fine."

Clint walked over to the cell. Andrew was standing right in front, holding tightly to the bars. Isobel and the sheriff would be able to hear what they said.

"Andrew," he said, "do you know me?"

"No, *señor*," the young man said. "Are you here to help me?" He looked scared out of his wits.

"Maybe I am," Clint said. "But it's important that you tell the sheriff and your sister that you don't know me."

Andrew looked past him and said, "I do not know this man!"

Hendricks exchanged a glance with Isobel.

"Do you believe him?" he asked.

"*Sí*," she said. "Andrew does not lie to me."

"*Señor*," Andrew said to Clint, "who are you?"

"My name is Clint Adams."

Andrew took a few steps back.

"B-But . . . you are not."

"Yes, I am."

"But . . . I have met Clint Adams," Andrew said. "I—I know him. H-He shot Joe Widmar."

"That's what he's been sayin'," Hendricks said. "That he didn't kill Widmar, you did."

"Not him," Andrew said. "Clint Adams."

Hendricks looked at Clint.

"Can you prove you're who you say you are?" the lawman asked.

"I've got some correspondence in my saddlebags," Clint said.

"Go get it."

Clint went out to Eclipse, got some letters from his saddlebags, and brought them back in. The sheriff looked them over, and handed them back.

"As far as I can tell," he said to Andrew," this man is Clint Adams, the Gunsmith."

"B-But . . ." Andrew said, "then who was the man who told me he was Clint Adams?"

"That's what I'd like to find out," Clint said. "Sheriff, you can let him out now."

"What makes you say that?" Hendricks asked.

"Well, it's obvious somebody had this kid convinced he was me."

"So? That don't mean this kid didn't kill Joe Widmar."

"Well, if the other man lied—"

"It don't make him a killer," Hendricks said. "I'm keepin' this kid until somebody can prove to me he didn't do it. Or until he goes to trial."

"But . . . this is the real Gunsmith," Isobel said.

"That's real nice," Hendricks said. "Maybe he can help you prove your brother's innocent. Until somebody does, he stays in my cell."

ELEVEN

The sheriff allowed Clint and Isobel to talk to her brother, but first he took Clint's gun.

"He told me his name was Clint Adams," Andrew said. "Did some target shooting to prove it."

"Was he good?"

"He didn't miss," Andrew said. "I believed him."

"What happened after that?"

"He said he needed a partner," Andrew said, "and we needed money."

"We?"

"Isobel and me," Andrew said.

"How much did he say he'd give you?"

"Five thousand dollars."

"For what?"

"He just said he wanted me to . . . back him up."

"Watch his back?"

"*Sí*, that was it. Watch his back."

"Did you have a gun, Andrew?"

"Yes."

"A pistol?"

"*Sí.*"

"You any good with it?"

"I can hit what I shoot at."

"But you never shot at a man."

Andrew hesitated.

"I already told him, *hermano*," Isobel said.

"No, I have never shot a man."

"Did you tell him that?"

"No."

"But I'll bet he knew."

"Then why did he—"

"Obviously, he didn't want somebody to watch his back," Clint said. "He wanted a patsy."

"A 'patsy'?"

"He wanted someone to blame when he killed Joe Widmar."

"Oh," Andrew said, "I see."

"Did he tell you who Widmar was?" Clint asked.

"No."

"So you just went with him . . . where?"

"To the man's house."

"And what happened?"

"He went inside," Andrew said. "I remained outside. Then I heard a shot."

"And you ran in."

"*Sí.*"

"With your gun out."

"*Sí.*"

"And something hit you on the head."

"How did you know that?"

"Not my first rodeo," Clint said.

"Excuse me?"

"I've heard this before. When you woke up, the sheriff was there?"

"Yes, and he arrested me."

"How long did you know the man?"

"Adams?" Andrew asked. "I mean, the man who said he was Adams?"

"Yes."

"It was just that day."

"One day?"

"Yes."

"He spotted you right away."

"What do you mean?" Isobel asked.

"I mean he picked your brother out as his patsy right away," Clint said.

"H-How did he do that?"

"He's probably good at it," Clint said.

"You have to find him," Andrew said. "He is the real killer."

"Did you ever see him with anyone else?" Clint asked.

"No, why?"

"Because maybe he had a friend who knew his real name."

"No, I did not see—but wait."

"What?"

"When I met him, he was in the saloon, drinking."

"And?"

"And talking to the bartender."

"Okay," Clint said. "Do you know the bartender's name?"

"No."

"Can you describe him to me?"

"*Sí.*"

"Okay," Clint said. "Describe the bartender to me, and then describe this phony Clint Adams to me."

"You will find him?"

"You will help us?" Isobel asked.

Clint looked at both of them and said, "I'm going to try."

TWELVE

"The kid never told me about no bartender," Sheriff Hendricks said.

"Well, he told me," Clint said. "Maybe you should question him."

"You know somethin'?" Hendricks asked.

"What?"   •

"I have my man, and he is set to go to trial," the lawman said. "It's up to you to try to prove that he's innocent."

"No help from you, huh?"

"Not my job," Hendricks said.

"You don't believe the kid at all?"

"Again," Hendricks said, "not my job. That's up to a lawyer."

"Does he have a lawyer?"

"Not that I know of."

"Okay," Clint said, "okay. Thanks . . . for nothing."

"Don't mention it."

* * *

Isobel was waiting for him outside.

"So?"

"He's not going to help."

"*Cabron!*"

"It's okay, Isobel," Clint said. "I'll do what I can."

"When?"

"As soon as I get a hotel room."

"I have a room," she said.

"Does Andrew have a room?"

"*Sí.*"

"Separate from you?"

"Yes."

"Good. I'll use his while he's in jail."

"All right."

"Do you have a key to his room?"

"The keys are at the hotel."

"Okay," Clint said. "Let's go. I also have to take care of my horse—and yours."

Right at that moment Isobel's horse keeled over and hit the ground. The buggy almost went with it. Clint could see from where he was that the animal was dead.

"We'll have to get somebody to move that," he said.

Clint took Eclipse to the livery, arranged with the liveryman to have Isobel's dead horse taken off the street.

"Does she need another one?" the man asked.

"Probably, but not right now."

"Well, come and see me when she does. I'll give ya a good price."

"Her," Clint said, "you'll give her a good price."

"Yes."

"And take good care of mine."

"Definitely," the man said. "Best-lookin' animal I ever seen."

"I'll be at the hotel."

"Which one?"

"This town have more than one?"

"Two."

"Well," Clint said, "I'll be at one of them."

"Okay."

Clint grabbed the man's arm as he started to turn away.

"He better be here, and all right, when I come to get him."

"Uh, okay," the man said. "Yeah, sure thing."

Clint walked outside, where Isobel was waiting.

"Now?" she asked. "Now can we look for the man?"

"Now," Clint said, "I will look for the man."

"I want to go with you."

"No," Clint said, "not to a saloon, and not to where I may have to go."

"But—"

"Come on," he said. "Let's get me Andrew's key, and get you to your room."

"And a bath."

"Yes," he said, "and a bath—for both of us."

She stared at him.

"I mean . . . we probably each need a bath."

"*Sí*," she said.

THIRTEEN

Of the two hotels in Tubac, Isobel and Andrew had rooms in the smaller one. The hotel had bathtubs, though, and they both made use of them. Clint went back to his room—Andrew's room—when he was done. He put on a fresh shirt he had in his saddlebags, and left the room. He walked down the hall and knocked on the door of the room next to his.

Isobel answered, her hair wet from her bath. She was holding her shirt closed with both hands.

"Just wanted to make sure you're okay," he said.

"I am fine."

"I'm going to go and ask some questions," he said. "It'd be better if you stayed in this room."

"But—"

"I'll come back and tell you what I find out," he said, cutting her off. "I promise."

She relented, said, "Very well."

He nodded, started to leave, then turned back and took her derringer from his belt.

"You might need this," he said, handing it back.

Tubac had two hotels, and two saloons. Clint wondered if it had two of everything.

He went into the first saloon he came to, took a good look at the bartender. Andrew had told him that the barman who had talked to the phony Clint Adams was a big, beefy man. This one was tall and reed thin.

"What can I getcha?" the man asked.

"You got another bartender works here?" Clint asked. "Big, beefy guy?"

"Not here," the man said. "Across the street. Sounds like you're looking for Bowe."

"Bow?"

"B-O-W-E," the man said. "Bowe. Bartender across the street."

"Thanks."

Across the street several men were standing at the bar when Clint walked in. They all turned to look at him. This saloon was bigger than the other one, but just as empty, except for the three men at the bar.

And the beefy bartender.

"Beer," Clint said.

"Comin' up," the man said.

The bartender set a cold mug in front of him. He picked it up and drained half of it.

"Been on the trail long?" one of the other men asked him.

"Long enough to need a cold beer."

"You look pretty clean to have come off the trail," a second man said.

"I took the time to get a bath," Clint said. "You might try it sometime."

The other men laughed at the joke. The butt of the joke scowled.

"Take it easy," Clint said. "I'm just kidding. Bartender, beers for my friends."

"Now yer talkin'," the first man said.

The bartender set them all up.

"How about you?" Clint asked.

"Sure."

The bartender got himself a beer, drank half of it.

"Got a minute?" Clint asked him.

"What for?"

"You Bowe?"

"That's right."

"Can we talk?"

Bowe looked at the other men.

"Go sit at a table," he told them.

They obeyed without question.

"My name's Clint Adams," Clint said. "That ring a bell?"

"Oh, yeah."

"Do you know me?"

"Never met you before."

"There was a man here a few days ago, claiming to be me."

"Not that I know."

"Okay, let me put it this way," Clint said. "He was seen in here talking to you."

"I talk to a lot of people," Bowe said. "What's he look like?"

Clint gave him the description Andrew had given to him.

"Kinda sounds like you," Bowe said.

"Yeah, it does."

The man rubbed his jaw, drank some more beer.

"Sounds like it could be Jess Mitchell."

"Who's he?"

"Sometime gunman, sometime bank robber," Bowe said.

"Is he wanted?"

"Not around here."

"Good with a gun."

"Handy, I'd say."

"That's what I heard. Friend of yours?"

"Customer."

"That's all?"

"That's it."

"Know where I can find him?"

"Nope."

"Know if he's still in Tubac?"

"Nope."

"Seen him in the last day or so?"

"No."

"He was in here with a young Mexican man," Clint said. "You remember that?"

"We talkin' about the kid in jail?" Bowe asked. "Killed Joe Widmar?"

"He says Mitchell did it," Clint said, "while he was pretending to be me."

"Now why would he do that?"

"I don't know. Did you know Widmar?"

"Everybody knew Joe," Bowe said. "He had a store in town."

"What kind of store?"

"Feed and grain."

"And he lived outside of town?"

"Right."

"Where he was killed."

Bowe shrugged.

"Okay, thanks," Clint said.

"Why are you lookin' for Mitchell?" Bowe asked.

"I don't like people impersonating me," Clint said. "Also, he framed an innocent kid for murder."

"So what are you gonna do?"

"I'm going to find him," Clint said, "and prove he killed Widmar, get that kid out of jail."

"That's all?"

Clint smiled, finished his beer, and set the empty mug on the bar.

"That's a start," he said.

FOURTEEN

Clint caught Hendricks coming out of his office.

"Oh, Adams," the sheriff said.

"Leaving the kid alone in there, Sheriff?" Clint asked.

"Deeds is with him."

"That deputy of yours strikes me as being pretty mean."

"He does his job," Hendricks said. "Were you comin' here lookin' for me?"

"I've got one question," Clint said. "You know a man named Mitchell, Jess Mitchell?"

"Yeah, I know Mitchell," Hendricks said. "Came to town a couple of weeks ago. Why?"

"Well, all I did was ask a few questions, but I think Mitchell's the man who was impersonating me."

"That may be, but it don't mean he killed Widmar instead of this kid."

"Well, whether he killed Widmar or not, I'm not about to let him keep on being me."

"That mean you're gonna kill 'im?"

"I'm going to stop him," Clint said. "How I do it will be up to him."

"Well, I don't want any more trouble in Tubac, Adams," Hendricks said. "I've had one murder too many already."

"There's not going to be another murder, Sheriff," Clint said.

"I'll hold you to that," Hendricks said.

Clint watched as the lawman walked away. If he did have to kill Jess Mitchell, he'd have to make sure it couldn't be called murder.

He waited for the sheriff to be out of sight, then went into the jailhouse.

"What are you doin' here?" Deputy Deeds asked.

"Just want to talk to the prisoner."

"The sheriff ain't here."

"I know, I saw him outside."

"He said it was okay?"

"We talked," Clint said, hoping that would be good enough for the deputy.

"Mister," Deeds asked, "you really Clint Adams?"

"That's right."

Deeds licked his lips.

"Well, okay, you can talk to 'im . . . five minutes!" he finally said.

"Sure, Deputy," Clint said, "five minutes."

Clint walked to his desk and set his gun down on it. He kind of wished he still had Isobel's derringer in his belt.

He walked to the cell, and Andrew came to the front to meet him.

"*Señor*, you have news?" he asked.

"Some, maybe," Clint said. "I figure the man you've been talking about is called Jess Mitchell. That sound familiar to you?"

"No," Andrew said. "I have never heard that name."

"Okay," Clint said, "I guess I'll just have to find him and bring him in here for you to have a look at."

"I will identify him, *señor*," Andrew said. "You can depend on it."

"All right, Andrew," Clint said. "Just sit tight, try not to worry."

"That is easy for you to say, *señor*."

"Yeah, you're right," Clint said. "It is. But try to do it anyway."

He retrieved his gun from the desk and left the jail.

From the sheriff's office, Clint went back to the hotel, knocked on Isobel's door. When she answered, she was fully dressed, and her hair was dry.

"Clint—"

"Can I come in?"

"Of course."

She backed away to allow him to enter. He closed the door, then looked at her.

"Would you like me to keep the door open?"

"Do not be silly," she said. "I trust you."

"That sounds odd, since it was only yesterday that you shot me."

"I am sorry about that," she said, ducking her head. "I was foolish." She looked at him. "Did you find the man?"

"I got a name," Clint said. "Jess Mitchell. I think he's the one."

"Where is he?"

"That's the problem," he said. "I'm still going to have to find him."

"Alone?"

"That's how it looks, unless . . ."

"Unless what?"

"Well, do you think your father will help? If you asked him?"

"I do not think my brother would want to ask him," she said. "And he would not want me to. To tell you the truth, I do not think my father would agree."

"What about the vaqueros at your father's ranch?" Clint asked. "Doesn't Andrew have any friends there?"

"They are all loyal to my father," she said. "They would not do anything without him."

"That's too bad. I get the feeling this sheriff would bend to any show of force."

"Could you force him to let my brother go?"

"I wouldn't want to go up against the law like that, Isobel," he said. "If your father rode in with some men, though, I think the sheriff would think twice."

"I would have to ride a long way to ask him," she said. "And then it would take time to come back, even if he agreed. Perhaps if you went and asked him. He would respect you."

"I better find out when this trial is likely to take place," Clint said. "Then we can make up our minds."

"I will come with you."

"No," he said, "I'm just going over to City Hall to find out when the judge is going to hold the trial. I'll come back and let you know."

"It is just that waiting here is . . . difficult."

"I can imagine," he said. "Look, I'll come back later and we'll go and get something to eat."

"Then can we bring something to my brother? I don't know how well they're feeding him."

"I'm sure the sheriff would agree to that, Isobel," Clint said. "We'll do it."

"Thank you, Clint."

"I'll be back soon."

Impulsively, she got up on her toes and kissed his cheek.

FIFTEEN

When Clint presented himself at City Hall, he was allowed in to see Mayor Stoffer.

"Well," Stoffer said when Clint entered his office, "what brings the Gunsmith to town?"

"I heard I was already in town," Clint said. "That is, an imposter was here."

"Really?" Stoffer asked. "If there was a man in town impersonating you, I certainly never heard about it. Did you talk to the sheriff?"

"I did," Clint said. "He also knows nothing about it."

"Well, what can I do for you, then?"

"I'm here about young Andrew Escalante."

"The man who killed Joe Widmar?"

"You mean the man accused of killing Joe Widmar, don't you?"

"I guess a jury will decide that."

"That's what I came here to find out," Clint said. "When is this trial supposed to take place?"

"As soon as the circuit judge gets to town."

"And when will that be?"

"As soon as he gets to town," the mayor said.

That was actually good news to Clint's ears. The boy may have to sit in a cell for weeks, but it would give Clint plenty of time to do what he had to do.

"And what's the judge's name?"

"Poindexter," Stoffer said. "Ever hear of him?"

"No."

"He hates Mexicans."

"Guess that's too bad for the kid, huh?"

"Very bad."

"What about a lawyer?"

"What about it?"

"The kid needs one."

Stoffer shrugged. He was a tall, well-built man in his fifties. Probably figured he'd look good in three-piece suits in Washington.

"Then he should get one," Stoffer said.

"Maybe I'll get him one, then."

Stoffer laughed.

"Just do him a favor," he said.

"What's that?"

"Make sure the lawyer's not Mexican."

"Do you know any lawyers in Mexico?" Clint asked Isobel later.

They were in a small café, waiting for their steak dinners.

"My father has several lawyers," she said.

"Well, Andrew's going to need one," Clint said. "Pick one."

"I do not need to," she said. "None of them will represent Andrew unless my father says it is all right. Except for one."

"Who's that?"

"Frederico Rodriguez."

"Will we have to go there and get him, or can we send a telegram?"

"A telegram will do."

"And he'll come?"

"Oh yes."

"Why?"

"He is the newest lawyer working for my father," she said. "And he's the youngest. He has a mind of his own, unlike the others, who have worked for my father for a long time."

"Why would your father hire a lawyer who has a mind of his own?" Clint asked. "He sounds like the kind of man who needs a bootlicker."

"He has all the bootlickers that he needs," she said. "He needed one man who could think, and who has a modern education."

The dinners came, steaming plates of meat and potatoes. The waiter set them down and scurried away.

"Tell me something," Clint said, cutting into his inch-thick steak.

"What is that?"

"Why do I have the feeling there's something you're not telling me?"

"About what?"

"About this lawyer, Fred."

"Frederico."

"Yeah, whatever."

She cut a small piece of steak, lifted it to her mouth on the end of the fork, but did not put it in.

"Well, there is one other thing."

"And what's that?"

She popped the piece of steak into her mouth.

"Frederico is in love with me."

SIXTEEN

The next morning Clint and Isobel had breakfast together, and then he accompanied her to the telegraph office. Frankly, he was surprised that a town the size of Tubac had one, but there it was.

"Frederico has his office in Nogales," she told Clint, "on the Mexican side."

"Fine," Clint said, "we'll send it there."

"What shall I say?" she asked.

If he was truly in love with her, the telegram probably only needed one line.

"Just tell him 'I need you,'" he told her. "That should do it, right?"

"Probably."

They entered the telegraph office and he let her write the message down and hand it to the clerk.

"Will you wait for an answer?" he asked.

"No," Clint said, "we're at the hotel . . . what's the name of it?"

"The Tubac Hotel."

"That's original," Clint said. He looked at the clerk.

"Got it," the man said.

Clint and Isobel walked out.

"What do we do now?" she asked as they walked down the street.

"I've got to find Mitchell," Clint said. "That means you go back to your room."

"But—"

"Somebody's got to wait for the answer from Freddy," he said.

"Frederico."

"Right," Clint said. "If he leaves right away, he should be here tomorrow, right?"

"Yes."

"Then you wait," Clint said. "If I'm not here when he gets here, you can tell him what's going on."

"What is going on?" she asked. "What will you want him to do?"

"If I can't find Jess Mitchell," Clint said, "then your Freddy is going to have to defend Andrew."

Clint actually had two things to do. He wanted to find Mitchell, and he wanted to get some information on Judge Poindexter.

He went back to the telegraph office, wrote out a message of his own, then sent to his friend Rick Hartman, in Labyrinth, Texas. If anyone could dig up information on the judge, it was Rick. He had connections all over the country.

"Send the reply to the hotel, like the other one?" the clerk asked.

"Yes, but this one goes to me," Clint said. "If I'm not there, leave it at the desk."

"Yessir."

He left the telegraph office and stood just outside, hands on hips. The question was where to look for Jess Mitchell? In a town as small as Tubac, that really shouldn't have been a problem.

He could have—and probably should have—left Tubac, and Arizona. The only way he could have done that quickly was to leave the country.

Nogales.

Mexico.

SEVENTEEN

"Are you sure?" Isobel asked. "Are you sure he's in Mexico?"

"No," Clint said, "but where else would he go? Just in case Andrew convinced the law that he was the actual killer, nobody could go into Mexico after him."

"Except for you."

"Right."

They were back at the café, this time for coffee and some talk.

"Did you get an answer from Freddy?" he asked.

"Frederico," she said. "He's on his way. He'll be here by morning. He promised."

"That's good. He can work on the case here, while I go look for Mitchell."

"But how will you find him?"

Clint shrugged.

"I'll just go to Nogales, see if anyone has seen him," Clint said. "If not, I'll come back here."

"Will you go see my father?"

"I hadn't thought of that," Clint said. "Why?"

"He would respect you," she said. "Respect who you are."

"Does that mean he'd come here and help?"

"I don't know," she said. "He was very hurt when we left."

"He might leave his son to die," Clint said, "but what if you were in danger? His daughter?"

"No," she said, shaking her head, "he would not come to save me. His son would be more important than his daughter."

"Then he wouldn't come to save either of you."

"Not on his own."

"What about your stepmother? Could she convince him?"

"I do not know," she said. "He is a proud man. But she does have some influence with him."

"All right," he said, "but first I'll be going to Nogales on this side of the border. If I go to the Mexican side, maybe I'll stop and see your father."

"And what about Andrew?" she asked. "What if Frederico can't help him? What if they decide to hang him?"

"It looks to me like they want to do this legally," Clint said. "If the judge should arrive and they start the trial, send me a telegram in Nogales. I can be back here quickly."

"I wish you did not have to go," she said.

"I'll stay tomorrow to meet Freddy," Clint said. "And I'll look around some more today. Tubac is not very big. If Mitchell is hiding in town, somebody should have seen him."

"What about outside of town?"

"There are some houses nearby," Clint said, "but who would be hiding him? He only arrived here a short while ago. Not enough time to make those kinds of friends."

Suddenly, something occurred to him. She noticed the look on his face.

"What are you thinking?"

"Joe Widmar."

"The man Andrew is in jail for killing?"

He nodded.

"His house is empty."

"You think this man Mitchell might be hiding there?" she asked.

"It's worth a look," he said. "Come on, I'll take you back to the hotel and then go check it out."

"Alone?" she asked as they stood up.

"Who would you suggest I take along?" he asked.

"Me."

"This could be dangerous, Isobel."

"I shot you, didn't I?"

"Good point," he said. "Okay. Let's get you a horse."

EIGHTEEN

They rode out to the Widmar house together. When they got there, they dismounted and Clint handed Isobel his .25 caliber Colt New Line.

"It's small, but bigger than your derringer," he said.

"Thank you."

"Let's go."

They approached the house on foot.

"Stay behind me," he said as they got closer.

When they reached the door, he directed her to one side, and he stood to the other. The house was small, probably two rooms and no other door.

"I'll go in first."

She nodded, held her gun ready.

He reached for the door handle and pushed the door open. He stepped inside, heard Isobel enter behind him.

"Watch yourself," he said.

This room was a combination kitchen and sitting room. The other room would be a bedroom.

"Watch the door," Clint said.

He went into the other room, found that it was, indeed, a bedroom. And it had recently been slept in.

He went back into the main room.

"I think he was here," he said. "Looks like somebody slept here since Widmar's death."

"So he's gone?"

"Looks like it, but let's go outside. I want to look around."

"For what?"

"Tracks."

They went outside.

"Keep a sharp eye out while I examine the ground."

"All right."

She looked around nervously while Clint walked about, staring down at the ground.

"There were horses here before us," he said. "Probably the sheriff and his deputy."

"And Mitchell?"

"If his horse was here, I can't tell it from the others."

"Then this was useless?"

"Not necessarily," Clint said. "Let's go back to town. I want to take a look at the sheriff's and the deputy's horses."

They mounted up and rode back to town.

"You want to what?" Sheriff Hendricks asked.

"I want to see your horse, and your deputy's."

"What for?"

"I want to see what tracks they leave."

"Why?"

"So I can eliminate them."

The sheriff didn't know what he was talking about, but didn't care.

"Our horses are at the livery. Go ahead and look at them, if you want. Tell Riker I said it was okay."

The liveryman, Riker, showed Clint where the sheriff's and the deputy's horses were. He stood by and watched while Clint examined their hooves.

"What're you lookin' for?" Riker asked.

"I just want to be able to know these tracks when I see them."

"You gonna be trackin' somebody?"

"I hope so," Clint said. "Thanks for your help."

He went outside, where Isobel was waiting.

"Did that help?"

"Yeah, it did," he said.

"Are we going back to the house?"

"I'll go back tomorrow. It'll be dark soon."

He walked their horses into the livery and left them in Riker's care. So far the man had done right by Eclipse.

"Ready to buy a new horse for the lady?" Riker asked.

"Not yet," Clint said. "I'll let you know when."

"Okay."

He went back outside, walked with Isobel back to the hotel.

Later that night, while he was sitting on the bed reading, she knocked at his door. He answered, gun in hand just in case.

"Isobel."

"I'm frightened," she said.

"Of what?"

"I do not know."

"Come in."

She hesitated.

"It's all right," he said. "You can have the bed. I'll sit in the chair."

She came in.

"I won't stay all night," she said, sitting on the bed.

"Okay."

"Just until I stop being frightened."

"Okay," he said again.

She reclined on the bed and fell asleep. He'd had women come to his room many times, but Isobel wasn't like any of those women. He knew she had only come because she was afraid. So he spent the night in a chair.

NINETEEN

Clint woke the next morning, lying in the bed beside Isobel. They were both fully dressed. He remembered her coming to him in the middle of the night, rousing him, and leading him to the bed.

"Go to sleep," she'd told him.

They'd both gone to sleep.

Now he sat up, rubbed his face vigorously. Isobel had to go back to her own room before Freddy the lawyer arrived. After all, he was in love with her, and they wouldn't want him to get the wrong idea.

"Isobel," he said.

"Hmm?"

"Time to get up," he said. "Freddy's going to be here soon."

She sat up quickly, looked around, and said, "*Madre de Dios!*"

"Nothing happened, Isobel," he said. "You just wanted to sleep here. Why don't you go back to your room and freshen up? We'll go have some breakfast. Maybe he'll be here by then."

"*Sí*," she said. "Thank you, Clint. I felt safe here last night."

"I'll meet you in the lobby."

Isobel looked very fresh and clean when she came down to the lobby. As a woman traveling, Clint assumed she had a trunk of clothes in her room. She was wearing a dress he had not seen yet.

He was wearing a fresh shirt, his last. He'd have to buy more.

"Ready for breakfast?" he asked.

"Yes, I'm—" She stopped and looked past him. He turned, saw a young Mexican man enter. He was wearing a dark suit that was covered with trail dust. He looked like a man who had ridden all night.

"Isobel?"

"Frederico!"

She rushed into his arms, and he embraced her but stared at Clint over her head. Clint thought Isobel might have been trying to deflect the man away from the fact that he'd found her with another man—even if they were only standing in the hotel lobby.

"Who is this man?" he demanded.

"This is Clint Adams," she said, putting just a little distance between them so she could turn and indicate Clint. "He's trying to help us."

"How?"

"Don't you mean 'why'?" Clint asked.

"Are you a lawyer?"

"No," Clint said, "you're the lawyer. That's why you're here."

"Isobel," Frederico said, "I came because you said you needed me."

"I do, Frederico," she said. "Andrew needs you."

"What is going on?"

"You look like you could use a hot meal and some coffee," Clint said. "Why don't we go someplace, sit down, and talk."

He could see the young lawyer wanted to get into it immediately, but in the end he gave in to his hunger, and the need for coffee.

"Very well," he said.

"Come," Isobel said, taking his hand. They walked that way together, ahead of Clint, to the café.

TWENTY

Over breakfast, Isobel told Frederico what had happened to Andrew. When she got to the part where she shot Clint, he took over the story.

"Wait," the lawyer said. "She actually shot you?"

"In the shoulder," Clint said, "with a small-caliber derringer."

Frederico looked at her.

"The one I gave you?"

"Yes," she said, casting her eyes downward.

"And you didn't have her arrested?"

"No," Clint said. "I didn't see the need."

He continued his story, all the way up to finding tracks at the home of the dead man.

"Now that I've seen the tracks left by the sheriff and deputy, I'm going to try to track Mitchell."

"What if the tracks aren't his?"

"That's a chance I'll take," Clint said. "It would help if the tracks lead south."

"Mexico?"

"I'm thinking that's where Mitchell would have to go until this blows over. Until the trial is over. It would also help him if Andrew was hanged."

Isobel grabbed Frederico's forearm.

"You have to keep that from happening, Frederico. Please."

"Have you spoken with Don Alfredo?"

"No."

"Why not?"

"You know why not."

"But . . . Andrew is his son."

"You know how Father feels about us leaving," she said.

"Hey, Fred," Clint said, "do you think you could talk her father into helping?"

The lawyer gave Clint a hard stare.

"My name is Frederico," he said, "and I hold no sway over Don Alfredo."

"What about some of his other lawyers?"

"They would not listen to me either."

"Well," Clint said, "I guess it's up to you, then. You have to defend him."

"When is the trial to start?"

"As soon as the circuit judge arrives. The mayor says it could be weeks."

Frederico looked at Isobel.

"I cannot stay here for weeks, Isobel."

"Frederico—"

"She could send you a telegram when the trial date is set," Clint said.

Frederico didn't speak.

"Or are you too afraid of her father to defend her brother . . . Freddy?"

"My name is Frederico," he said, "and I am not afraid of Don Alfredo. But I am loyal to him."

"And he wouldn't want you to help Andrew, right?"

Instead of answering Clint, Frederico looked at Isobel.

"*Querida*, I must talk with your father about this, about us."

"You will be going back to Mexico?"

"Of course."

"But you will talk to Andrew first?"

He reached out and took her hands.

"Yes, of course. I will talk to him, and reassure him."

"Good," she said. "Thank you, Frederico."

The lawyer looked at Clint.

"I do not think we will need your help," he said.

"Oh, well, that's not for you to say, Freddy," Clint replied. "I promised Isobel I'd help her brother."

"I am here now," the lawyer said. "She does not need you."

"Well, there's still the part about Mitchell impersonating me," Clint said. "I can't let him go on doing that. So whether you like it or not, I'm going to stick with this."

"Stick?"

Clint leaned forward and said, "I'm not going to stop until I catch Jess Mitchell."

"If he brings this man back," Isobel said, "it will help Andrew."

"Yes," Frederico said, "very well."

"And since you're going back to Mexico," Clint said, "we might as well travel together. Especially if you're go-

ing to be talking to Don Alfredo. I'd like to talk to him myself."

"I pushed my horse hard," the Mexican said. "It will
have to rest. I cannot leave until tomorrow."

"Well, I'll take another look at those tracks out at the
Widmar house," Clint said. "I might be able to wait until
tomorrow myself."

"I cannot guarantee Don Alfredo will talk to you."

"That's okay," Clint said. "I'll take care of that part myself. How about some more coffee?"

TWENTY-ONE

While Isobel took Frederico over to the sheriff's office, Clint rode back out to the Widmar house. He dismounted, careful not to trample the tracks he was interested in. He studied them, was able to isolate the sheriff's horse, and then the deputy's. It looked to him like there was one set of tracks left.

He walked around to the back of the house, found a single set of tracks. They matched the third set from the front. So if Jess Mitchell had spent a night or two here, these tracks belonged to his horse.

Clint decided to follow them for a while, until he was sure what direction they were going.

Within two hours he became convinced that Mitchell was riding for Mexico. Or, at least, Nogales. Now he had to decide if he wanted to follow him right away, or wait until the next day, when Freddy the lawyer headed back to Mexico.

* * *

Clint went back to Tubac.

He figured whether Jess Mitchell was in Nogales in the United States, or Nogales in Mexico, he'd stay there. As far as the man knew, nobody was looking for him.

Clint entered the hotel, with the intention of going up to Isobel's room, but instead he stopped at the desk.

"Yes, sir?" the clerk asked.

"*Señor* Frederico Rodriguez," Clint said. "Has he checked in?"

The clerk looked at the register and said, "Yes, sir, Mr. Rodriguez is in Room Number 8."

"Thanks."

He went upstairs and knocked on Isobel's door. When she opened the door, she looked tired.

"Is Freddy here?" he asked.

"No," she said, "Frederico has his own room, but I believe he is out."

"Can I come in?"

"Of course."

Inside the room he asked, "Did you and he talk to Andrew?"

"We did."

"And?"

"He has agreed to be Andrew's lawyer," she said. "But . . ."

"But he's still going to talk to your father before actually defending him."

"Yes."

"Is he going back to Nogales tomorrow?"

"Yes."

"Okay, I'll go with him, then."

"He does not like you."

"That's obvious."

"You keep calling him Freddy," she said. "You want him to dislike you."

"No," he said, "I just think he should loosen up a bit."

"I do not think that will happen," Isobel said. "Frederico is not . . . loose."

"Well, maybe I can loosen him up on the ride to Nogales."

"Please," she said, "do not hurt him."

"Why would I do that?"

"Frederico has a temper," she said. "He might do something . . . silly."

"Why would he do that?"

She didn't answer.

"Is he jealous?"

"Sí."

"But we haven't done anything to make him jealous," Clint said.

"He does not think so."

"Well, I'll have to straighten him out," Clint said. "Looks like we'll have an interesting ride to Nogales."

"Perhaps," she said, "you should resolve your issues even before that."

"You might be right," Clint said. "Maybe I should buy the young man a drink."

"Except," she said, "he gets angrier when he is drunk."

"I'll try my best not to get him drunk, then," Clint said. "Just loose."

She looked unhappy.

"I am not confident."

"Let me ask you this," he said. "Is he a good lawyer?"

"He is very good," she said. "He's smart and clever."

"Okay, then," Clint said. "I'll do my best to keep him happy."

"*Gracias*, Clint."

TWENTY-TWO

Clint found the young Mexican lawyer in the saloon, having a drink at the bar. He was wearing the same suit, but it had been brushed until it was almost spotless.

He stood next to Frederico and said, "I'll have a beer," to the bartender.

"Comin' up."

Frederico turned his head and looked at Clint.

"Hey, Freddy."

"Why do you insist on calling me that?" Frederico asked.

"Because you've got to relax," Clint said. "Freddy is a relaxing name. Frederico . . . that's too stiff."

"What do you want?" the Mexican lawyer asked.

"I'm going to ride to Nogales with you tomorrow," Clint said. "I'm convinced that's where I'll find Jess Mitchell."

"Fine," Frederico said, "as long as we do not talk along the way."

"Well, see," Clint said, "I thought we should talk now."

The bartender brought Clint a beer and Clint said, "Bring my friend another one, on me."

"Comin' up."

The place was about half full, but there were plenty of tables available. As the bartender brought Frederico's second beer, Clint grabbed both his and the lawyer's and said, "Come on, let's sit."

Clint walked to a table and set both beers down. Frederico resisted, but in the end he followed and sat in front of his fresh beer.

"What do you want, *señor*?"

"I'll tell you what I want," Clint said. "I want to find the man who was impersonating me. I want to help Isobel and Andrew prove that he's innocent of murder."

"That is all?"

"That is everything," Clint replied. "I understand you and Isobel have a relationship. She told me."

"She did?" Frederico asked. "What did she tell you?"

"She told me that you are in love with her."

"Did she say anything else?"

"What more do you want?"

Frederico sat back, shoulders slumped.

"She did not tell you that she is in love with me?" he asked.

"No, she didn't say that," Clint said. "But she didn't say she wasn't."

"And you are not in love with her?"

"Freddy," Clint said, "I'm a lot older than she is. No, I'm not in love with her."

"And you do not . . . desire her?"

"I only desire to help these two kids," Clint said, "because it looks like their father won't."

"He is a hard man, Don Alfredo," Frederico said.

"That's what Isobel told me."

"He wants Andrew to take over the ranch after he is gone," Frederico said, "but it does not look like that will happen."

"Because Andrew wants to be his own man?"

"No," the lawyer said, "it is because Andrew is not a strong man."

"Well, he's not a man, really," Clint said. "He's still young."

"Don Alfredo is not a very patient man," Frederico said. "He wants Andrew to be ready now."

"Well, that's too bad," Clint said. "Sometimes it takes a boy time to grow up."

"Don Alfredo is elderly," Frederico said. "He had his children late in life for him. He does not have that much time to wait."

"All the more reason he should stay on good terms with his children. Maybe you can talk some sense into him."

"I would not try," Frederico said.

"What about the other lawyers?"

"They are both lifelong friends with Don Alfredo," Frederico said. "They both fear him."

"His friends fear him?"

"*Sí, señor.*"

"And do you fear him?"

"No, I do not. But I do not discuss personal matters with him."

"Then there isn't anyone who can try to talk sense into him?"

"No, *señor*."

"Well," Clint said, "I guess I'll have to try."

"I wish you luck, *señor*," Frederico said. "I have never known Don Alfredo to listen to anyone."

"All I need from you is an introduction," Clint said. "Surely you'd be able to do that, wouldn't you? Frederico?"

The man hesitated, then said, "*Sí, señor.* I am able to do that."

"Good."

TWENTY-THREE

In Nogales, on the Mexican side, Jess Mitchell was enjoying himself.

It was all about whiskey, food, and women for him. He was staying in a room behind a small cantina, having food and whores brought into him.

At the moment he had a half-finished plate of tacos and beans on the table next to the bed while he plowed one of the whores from behind.

He had been rotating three women in and out of his bed. They were all Mexican, with dark skin, black eyes, and black hair, but in order to keep it interesting, one of them was nineteen, one was twenty-eight, and the other one was over forty.

The nineteen-year-old was, of course, the least experienced. He kept having her brought in mostly for what he could teach her. The twenty-eight-year-old was experienced and eager, but it was the older one—forty-five if she was a day—who had become his favorite. She had all the experience in the world, and would do anything.

At the moment she was letting him fuck her ass, which he hadn't even approached the other two girls about. The nineteen-year-old—Xena—would have been shocked at the suggestion. The middle girl, Rosa, might have gone for it, but he hadn't yet tried.

But the older woman, Helena, was ready for anything. Also, she had a lush body with big breasts and hips, while the other women were sleek and small breasted. Part of the reason for Helena's lushness was her age, of course. In a few years she might even be fat, but at the moment she was what Jess Mitchell liked to call "juicy."

He fucked her hard now, driving his hard cock into her, as she groaned and cried out, but her cries had nothing to do with pain. In fact, as he drove himself into her, she rammed her ass back against him so that they were actually both working very hard at this.

Or playing.

The bed frame was creaking, the room was filling with the scent of their sweat and her juices.

"Come on, *cabron*," she exhorted him.

He was already fucking her as hard as he could so he decided to slap her ass at the same time. Maybe that would satisfy her. This woman—of all the women he'd ever been with—was the hardest to satisfy, but it was a challenge he was happy to rise to.

He grabbed hold of her hips as he felt himself building toward his climax and then bellowed like a bull as he emptied into her.

He withdrew from her and she turned over onto her back, her big breasts flopping over to either side, the big, brown nipples still as hard as diamonds.

He leaned over and placed his face between her breasts, licking the sweat from her body. She pressed her breasts together, trapping his face there, then set him free so he could lick her nipples clean of perspiration.

After that he sat on the side of the bed, reached for a taco and the bottle of tequila on the table next to the bed.

"You have many appetites, Jess," she said. He liked the way the three whores pronounced his name. It sounded like they were saying "Yes."

"I've got an appetite for you, that's for sure," he said, slapping her on one meaty thigh.

"More than Xena and Rosa?" she asked. "They are so much younger than I am."

"They got nothin' on you, Helena," he said, grabbing one of her breasts and squeezing it. He got some sauce from the taco on her breast, so he leaned over and licked it off. Then he gave her the bottle of tequila so she could have a drink.

He got up and walked to the window. The room was on the main floor, and all he could see was an alley that ran alongside. He didn't mind having that room, since no one was looking for him. Still, he preferred to remain in the room as much as possible, coming out only occasionally to take a walk, stretch his legs, and maybe have a drink in the cantina. He was getting kind of tired of Xena and her lack of experience. Maybe, while in the cantina, he'd see another girl who would strike his fancy. He'd check it out later today, in fact.

"I must go to work," Rosa said, swinging her bare feet to the floor. "When will you want me again?"

"I'll let you know later," he said. "We don't want poor Helena getting jealous, do we?"

"She does not make you as happy as I do," she said.

"Yeah, well, you're the one who brings the food with you."

She laughed, donning her skirt and peasant blouse. The first time he saw her in that blouse, with her big, loose breasts spilling out, he knew he had to have her, no matter what her age was.

She put on her shoes and said, "Then I will see you in the cantina?"

"You bet."

He went over to her, kissed her soundly, and sent her from the room with a resounding slap on her ample butt.

When she was gone, he went back to the bottle of tequila and used it to wash down the rest of the tacos and beans that were on the plate.

He'd been in Nogales for several days. First, he had stopped in the U.S. side, but then he decided he'd be better off in Mexico. He was sure the kid he'd framed for Widmar's murder was going to swing for it, but he was playing it safe and staying in Mexico until it was all over.

The kid had been easy, and the stroke of genius had been to pretend to be Clint Adams, the Gunsmith. That had really impressed the boy.

He drained the tequila bottle, then decided to get dressed and go on out to the cantina now for a beer, and another bottle.

And maybe he'd bring one of the girls back with him. His dick was already getting hard again.

TWENTY-FOUR

Clint felt that he and Frederico had cleared the air. They left the saloon together, and the lawyer said he was going back to the hotel. Clint decided to go and have a talk with Andrew. If he was going to talk to the boy's father, maybe he'd be able to give him some advice.

"Back again?" Hendricks asked. "The other two were here a while ago."

"I'm leaving town tomorrow," Clint said. "I just want to talk to the kid before I go."

"Fine," Hendricks said. "Gun on the desk."

Clint placed his weapon on the desk and walked over to the cell. He noticed that Andrew remained on his cot, rather than rushing forward anxiously.

"Hey, kid."

"*Señor* Adams."

"Listen, Freddy and me are going to Nogales tomorrow."

"Freddy?" Andrew frowned.

"Your lawyer?"

"Oh, Frederico."

"Yes," Clint said.

"Why are you going there?"

"I think Mitchell is hiding out there," Clint said. "Also, I'm going to talk to your father."

"About what?"

"About you," Clint said. "Why else would I talk to him?"

"You are not going to change my father's mind about me," Andrew said. "I am simply not the man he wants me to be."

"You're not a man at all," Clint said. "You're still a boy."

"That is not how he feels."

"Well, maybe I can change his mind."

"You won't change his mind about Isobel and I leaving home."

"We'll see," Clint said. "I just wanted you to know I might be gone for a day or two."

"What if the trial starts?"

"It won't," Clint said. "It will take a while for the judge to get here. I should be back in plenty of time."

"What about Isobel?"

"She'll be here in town."

"And Frederico?"

"He's going back, too," Clint said. "He needs to talk to your father."

"To get permission to defend me."

"Yes."

"And if my father says no, he won't come back."

"Unless Isobel can get him to come back."

"His love for my sister will not overcome his loyalty to my father."

"Maybe not."

Andrew's head dropped and he stared at the floor.

"Thank you."

"For what?"

"For what you are trying to do."

"You just hang on, kid," Clint said. "I'm going to drag Mitchell back here and make him confess. And then you'll be out of here."

"I await that day," Andrew said.

Clint nodded, walked to the sheriff's desk to pick up his gun.

"You know there's talk," Hendricks said.

"What kind of talk?"

Hendricks looked over at Andrew, then lowered his voice and said, "Lynch talk."

"You won't allow that."

"You're right," he said. "I'd stop any lynch mob in my town . . . if I can."

"Are you telling me you don't think you'll be able to?"

"I'm just sayin'," Hendricks replied, "don't be away too long."

Clint left the sheriff's office with sudden second thoughts. If there was lynch talk in town, maybe it was better for him to stay. But that would not accomplish anything as far as clearing the kid. It would only keep him alive. For now.

And why a lynch mob? Was the dead man that well liked in town? Clint hadn't heard anything to that effect since his arrival.

No, if there was lynch talk, it probably didn't have much strength behind it. Lynch talk usually came from one man trying to rile up a crowd. Clint hadn't heard anything like that in town.

In the morning he and the lawyer would head to Nogales. If they left early enough, pressed on, and didn't stop, they'd make it by tomorrow night—at least to the U.S. side. Once there, he could talk to the sheriff, and see what the law knew. Then the next day they'd cross over to the Mexican side and—if nothing else—talk to Don Alfredo Escalante about his children.

TWENTY-FIVE

In the morning Clint pounded on Frederico's door. The man answered, stripped to the waist and looking bleary-eyed.

"Wha—"

"Time to go, Freddy."

Frederico rubbed his face with both hands and asked, "Breakfast?"

"Beef jerky and water," Clint said, "on the move. Come on, let's go. We want to get to Nogales by tonight."

"We do?"

"Yes, we do. Get dressed! I'll meet you in the lobby."

From the lobby Clint took a sleepy-eyed Frederico to the livery stable, where they saddled Eclipse and the lawyer's horse, a healthy-looking pinto.

Frederico looked at Clint's horse and said, "I cannot keep up to you on that."

"Your pinto will do fine. It's a good horse."

As they saddled the animals, Riker, the livery man, said,

"He's right. You go into any kind of run and that little pinto will never keep up."

"Not looking for speed," Clint said. "Just stamina. We're gonna walk all day. The pinto can keep up."

"Maybe," Riker said.

"I know horses," Clint said.

"So do I," Riker said. "Just walkin' next to your horse will ruin any other horse."

"We'll take it easy."

They walked the two horses outside and mounted up.

"You going to be able to stay in that saddle?" Clint asked him.

"I am fine," Frederico said. "Can we say good-bye to Isobel?"

"You'll see her in a few days," Clint said, "but yeah, we'll ride by the hotel."

As they rode by the hotel, Isobel appeared in the window of her room and looked down at them. Frederico waved to her and Clint nodded and said to the lawyer, "So let's ride."

Outside of Tubac they came upon the tracks Clint had been following.

"They head south," he said, pointing.

"What if it is not him?"

"Like I told you before," Clint said, "I believe Jess Mitchell is in Nogales, so whether these tracks are his or not, that's where I'm going."

"I do not understand your reasoning, *Señor* Adams."

"My reasoning is very simple," Clint said. "It's what I would do if I was him."

"I do not see how you can put yourself in the place of such a man," Frederico said. "I would not be able to do it."

"Well, you and me, we've lived very different lives, Freddy," Clint said. "I have dealt with men like this all my life. It's not hard at all for me to try and think like them."

"Well, I cannot understand it, but I am going to Nogales for my own purpose."

"Then let's get a move on. We might as well follow these tracks as far as they take us."

"I do not care," Frederico said. "I am going that way in any case."

They rode south for a few hours, and Clint was satisfied with the performance of Frederico's little pinto. Even Eclipse seemed happy with the smaller horse and seemed to be regulating his stride to accommodate the pinto.

Frederico, however, seemed to be suffering the effect of having already ridden hard from Nogales to Tubac once.

"I need to stop," he said at one point.

"I want to get to Nogales tonight, Freddy."

The man seemed to have given up on getting Clint to call him by his proper name.

"Then you may go on ahead," he said, reining in his horse and dismounting.

"You spend too much time in a court room and not enough time on a horse, Freddy," Clint said.

"Well, the courtroom is where I get paid to do my job."

"You don't want Isobel to be disappointed in you, do you? She's depending on you to save her brother."

Frederico bent over and put his hands on his knees,

seemed to be having trouble getting his breath. He stared up at Clint.

"Isobel knows that I work for her father," he said. "I cannot defend Andrew without Don Alfredo's approval."

"Did you tell Andrew that? So he's not depending on you?"

Frederico didn't answer.

"So he's sitting in a cell, expecting you to come back and defend him, and if Don Alfredo says no, you won't show up?"

"I have told you," Frederico said, "I work for Don Alfredo. My loyalty must be to him."

"And how do you think Isobel will feel about you when you've abandoned her brother?"

"She will understand," Frederico said. "She is going to be my wife. She will have to understand."

"Freddy," Clint said, "I'm afraid you don't know women very well."

"What do you mean?"

"Well," Clint said, "women don't have to do anything they don't want to do."

"She will be obedient."

"Like I said," Clint replied, "you don't know much about women."

He continued south with Eclipse at a brisk walk. Frederico stared after Clint for a few moments, then mounted up and started off after him.

TWENTY-SIX

They rode into Nogales soon after dark. It was a much larger town than Tubac. Frederico and his pinto had managed to keep up, but while the horse was in fine shape, the man was exhausted.

"Just lead me to a hotel, and you can go home and get some rest," Clint said.

"I do not live here, *señor*. I lived across the border. So we will both need a hotel."

"Fine," Clint said. "Where's the nearest one?"

"This way, *señor*."

They left their horses in the livery and then registered at the hotel, which was larger than Clint had expected.

"In the morning I'm going to talk to the sheriff," Clint said. "If he can't help me locate Jess Mitchell, I'll have to go across the border."

"I need to rest," Frederico said. "So you will be on your own tomorrow morning."

"Suits me," Clint said, and left Frederico standing in the lobby.

In the morning Clint didn't bother checking on Frederico. He was sure the young man was still asleep, trying to recover from his two days in the saddle.

He asked the desk clerk for a decent place for breakfast and had to walk down only two streets to get to it. It was a small cantina where he was able to get some good huevos rancheros, to which he got them to add some steak and tortillas. The food was good, the coffee was strong and black, the way he liked it.

After breakfast he walked around Nogales, found it busy in the morning. The people seemed friendly, as he exchanged some greetings with total strangers, both men and women. Eventually, he found himself in front of the sheriff's office, wondering if the lawman would be as friendly as the other folks in town. There was a shingle on the wall that said the sheriff's name was W. Stroby.

He opened the door and stepped in.

A man wearing a badge and a serious look glanced up from his desk.

"Help ya?" he asked.

"Sheriff Stroby?"

"It's Stroby," the man said, correcting Clint's pronunciation from a short "o" to a long one.

"Sorry, Sheriff Stroby," Clint said. "I just arrived in town last night and wanted to talk to you about something."

"What?"

"I'm looking for a man named Jess Mitchell," Clint said. "Might be guilty of a murder that took place in Tubac."

The sheriff sat back. His serious countenance made him appear older, but Clint guessed his age as mid-thirties.

"You a bounty hunter?"

"No, sir."

"Who are you?"

"My name's Clint Adams."

Stroby gave his jaw a hard run with his left hand.

"Don't know as if that's much better," he said. "What's the Gunsmith want with this Mitchell? You lookin' to kill 'im?"

"I'm looking to take him back to Tubac to stand trial," Clint said.

"You ain't wearin' a badge."

"No, I'm not."

"Why isn't the sheriff here?" Stroby asked. "Hendricks, ain't it?"

"That's right," Clint said. "Sheriff Hendricks has a man in custody for the murder, but it's the wrong man."

"And whose opinion is that?"

"Mine."

"So you got no authority here."

"No, sir, I don't," Clint said.

"So what's your interest?"

"Seems like Jess Mitchell was going by a different name in Tubac."

"What name was that?"

"Clint Adams."

"Ah," Stroby said, "I think I'm startin' to see your interest."

"I don't like anybody impersonating me," Clint said, "especially when they might be guilty of murder."

"Who says he did it?"

"The man the sheriff has in a cell."

"And you believe him?"

"Yes."

"When is Mitchell supposed to have left Tubac?"

"A few days ago. Don't know if he came directly here or not, but we followed some tracks that may have been his."

"We?"

"I rode in with a lawyer named Frederico Rodriguez," Clint explained.

Stroby raised his eyebrows in recognition.

"Now that name I do know," he said. "Works for Don Alfredo Escalante."

"That's right."

"What's his interest?"

"The man in jail in Tubac is Don Alfredo's son, Andrew."

Now Sheriff Stroby dry washed his face with both hands.

"This sounds like it's complicated."

"Extremely," Clint said. "Would it help you to know the whole story?"

"No," Stroby said, "but why don't you tell me anyway."

TWENTY-SEVEN

Clint told the sheriff the whole story. The man listened quietly, chin propped up on his hands.

"You're taking the word of both Isobel and Andrew that he didn't do it."

"Yes."

"Why?"

Clint shrugged. "I believe them."

"Have anything to do with the fact that she's pretty?" Stroby asked.

"Has more to do with the fact that she was mad enough to shoot me."

"Maybe Andrew's even lying to her," the lawman suggested.

"Could be," Clint said. "I'm reserving my final opinion until I can talk to Jess Mitchell."

"So you're leavin' room for the possibility that he wasn't impersonating you, and had nothin' to do with the killin'."

"If I've learned anything over the years, it's that anything's possible."

"I can believe that," Stroby said.

"So," Clint said, "you haven't said yet whether or not Mitchell is or was here."

Stroby tapped his fingers on the top of his desk and then said, "He was."

"When?"

"He rode in a few days ago," Stroby said.

"And stayed how long?"

"Until I kicked him out of town."

"What for?"

"He started a fight, almost killed a man."

"A fight over what?"

"A woman."

"Did he resist?"

"Nope," Stroby said, "and now I know why."

"He didn't want to have any trouble with the law if he could help it."

"Not if he was tryin' to hide out."

"So where did he go?" Clint asked. "Do you know?"

"I know he went across the border," Stroby said. "I don't know if he stopped in Nogales, or kept goin'."

"Well, that's a bit helpful anyway," Clint said, standing.

"You goin' across?" Stroby asked.

"Yep."

"Takin' young Rodriguez with you?"

"Yes."

"He gonna take you to see Don Alfredo?"

"I hope so."

"That's one stubborn old buzzard," Stroby said. "You

think you can convince him to help a son he doesn't approve of?"

"I hope so," Clint said. "Or maybe I can convince the boy's stepmother."

"I'll be very interested to see if you even get to talk to her."

"Any advice about handling Don Alfredo?"

"No," Stroby said, "except maybe talk to Sheriff Lopez when you get there."

"Is he a good man?"

"He's the sheriff," Stroby said. "That's about all I can say, but he's had more dealings with the old man than I have. Maybe he can give you some advice. His name's Hector Lopez."

"Good," Clint said. "I'll check in with him as soon as I get there."

"Mention my name, if you think it will do you any good," Stroby said. "I can't tell you if it really will or not."

"Thanks," Clint said. "I'll use it if I think I need to."

The sheriff stood and the two men shook hands.

"Stop by here on your way back," Stroby said. "I'd like to know how things went with the old man."

"I'll do it."

TWENTY-EIGHT

When Clint left the sheriff's office, he went to the hotel to see if the lawyer had awakened yet. He knocked on the man's door a couple of times, then went down to the desk clerk.

"Have you seen the man who checked in with me last night? Mr. Rodriguez?"

"Yes," the clerk said. "He went out about half an hour ago."

"Do you know where he was going?"

"No, sir."

"Okay, thanks."

Frederico would not have had to ask the clerk about a place for breakfast, since he had been to Nogales before. Maybe he went to have breakfast, or maybe he was doing something else. Could be he went to send a telegram, either to Tubac or to Nogales across the border.

Clint left the hotel and went looking for the telegraph office, just to check.

* * *

Frederico wasn't at the telegraph office, and the clerk would not give him any information.

"I don't talk about customers," the man said.

"That's admirable," Clint said, "but I don't want to know what his telegram said, I just want to know if he was here."

"What'd you say his name was?"

"Frederico Rodriguez," Clint said.

The clerk looked down, moved some papers around, then said, "Yeah, he was here a little while ago."

"Thanks," Clint said. "Then I'm on the right track. Don't suppose he said where he was going?"

"No," the clerk said, "but he did comment on how hungry he was."

"Is there a good place to eat near here?"

"Sure is," the man said. "Right around the corner. Get my lunch there every day myself."

"Does it have a name?"

"Naw, everybody knows where it is."

"Okay, thanks."

Clint left the telegraph office, walked around the corner, and found the little restaurant. He could see there was no name, but the word STEAKS was painted on the big front window. He peered in the window and saw the lawyer eating breakfast.

"Good morning," he said, presenting himself at the table. "Mind if I join you?"

"To be frank," Frederico said, "I was hoping you had left for Mexico."

Clint sat down, poured himself some coffee.

"Not without you, my friend," Clint said. "I hear you sent a telegram this morning."

Frederico frowned.

"How did—"

"I stopped around the corner," Clint said. "Who'd you send it to, Don Alfredo?"

"No," Frederico said, "I sent it to Manuel Ruiz. He is Don Alfredo's oldest friend, and has been his lawyer for many years."

"And what did you tell him?"

"That you would probably be coming to town tomorrow," Frederico said.

"Get an answer?"

"Not yet," the young lawyer said, "but I am sure he will want me to bring you to him first, before you try to see Don Alfredo."

"That's okay with me," Clint said.

"Did you have your talk with the sheriff?" Frederico asked.

"I did," Clint said. "He told me Jess Mitchell was here, but he ran him out of town."

"And where did he go?"

"Across the border."

Frederico made a face.

"So you're going across?"

"Definitely," Clint said, "and I thought we could go today instead of tomorrow."

"Today?" Frederico said. "When?"

"As soon as you finish eating." He drained his coffee cup and got up. "I'll go to the hotel and check us out, and meet you at the livery. There's nothing in your room, right?"

"Saddlebags—"

"I'll get them," Clint said. "Finish your breakfast and meet me at the horses."

"But—"

"Don't worry," Clint said. "I'll pay for the rooms." He started for the door, then turned back. "You can pay me back later."

TWENTY-NINE

Clint was starting to wonder if Frederico was going to show up at the livery when the lawyer walked in.

"About time, Freddy," he said. "Let's go."

He mounted up, held out the reins of the pinto to the lawyer. He was waiting for the young man to stand up to him, but instead he stepped forward, accepted the reins, and mounted up.

They rode out of Nogales on the U.S. side, headed for Nogales on the Mexican side.

Clint had been to towns like Nogales before. Split in two. Most notably El Paso, where both sides of the town were split by a bridge.

With Nogales there was no bridge. You were simply in the United States one moment, and Mexico the next. Nogales, Mexico, was in Sonora, and they still had to ride a way before they entered the town.

There was an attitude about Mexican towns. Clint knew

that if he'd been brought here blindfolded and then had the blindfold removed, he'd still know he was in Mexico. It was something in the air, an almost palpable difference— warmer, thicker, lazier.

They rode down the main street and encountered only a few men, no women.

"The town is asleep," Frederico said. "Siesta."

"I thought that was in the afternoon."

"It is all the time," Frederico said with some disgust.

"Where's your office?" Clint asked.

"I do not have my own office," he said. "I will take you to *Señor* Ruiz."

"That's fine. But we left before he could reply to your telegram."

"He will know we are coming," Frederico assured him.

They rode to an adobe building that stood two stories. There were some cracks in the walls, but it seemed solid enough.

They dismounted and left the horses out front. Frederico tied his pinto tightly to a post, but Clint only lopped Eclipse's reins around it. They went inside.

"I use that room," Frederico said, pointing. The door was closed. Clint had a feeling the room was the size of a closet.

They were in an outer office with some file cabinets and an empty desk that had dust on the top of it. Frederico took Clint past the desk to a door and knocked.

"Come!"

THIRTY

Frederico opened the door and led the way into the room. An older man stood behind a desk and regarded them. He was a small man, wizened, bent. Clint wondered if he was even as young as eighty.

"Manuel Ruiz," Frederico said, "this is Clint Adams, the Gunsmith."

"Yes," Ruiz said, "I received your telegram, Frederico. Why don't you leave *Señor* Adams here with me and let us talk? You probably have some files in your office to take care of."

"Yes," Frederico said, "yes, I do."

He hesitated, then left the room.

"Please, sit down, *señor*."

"Thank you."

"I understand you want to talk to Don Alfredo Escalante."

"Yes. Freddy tells me that you and he have been friends for a long time."

"Indeed."

"And you've been his lawyer . . ."

"For all that time," Ruiz said.

"Then maybe you can talk some sense into the man," Clint said.

"About what?"

"His children."

"What do you know of his children?"

"I know that his son is in jail in Tubac, charged with murder," Clint said. "And I know that his sister is so convinced that he didn't do it, she tried to kill the man she thought did do it."

"And who was that?"

"Me," Clint said. "She shot me in the shoulder with a small-caliber derringer."

"And you did not have her arrested?"

"She didn't need to be arrested," Clint said. "She needed help. Andrew needs help."

"And you are helping them?"

"I'm trying," Clint said, "but I think their father could help them a lot more than I could."

"What could Don Alfredo do about his son being in jail in the United States?" the lawyer asked. "Do you suggest he should break him out?"

"He has a lot of money," Clint said. "Money can buy almost anything in my country."

"And in mine," Ruiz said, "but Don Alfredo's children have walked away from him of their own accord. It was their own decision."

"They went out on their own, yes," Clint said. "There's a big difference between that and what he has done in disowning them, though."

"I am Don Alfredo's lawyer," Ruiz said. "I cannot tell him how to raise his children."

"His children have already been raised," Clint said. "Isobel's a woman, Andrew's a young man. But they still need him."

"And what do you think I can do?"

"Talk some sense into him."

Ruiz sat back in his chair.

"I think you might have the wrong idea of my relationship with Don Alfredo, *Señor* Adams," Manuel Ruiz said.

"I thought you were friends."

"Friendship," he said, "does not mean the same thing to him as it does to others. I am as much a friend to him as anyone could be. That does not mean I can talk to him about personal matters."

"Well," Clint said, "maybe I can."

"How do you propose to do that?"

"Either you or Freddy will take me to see him."

"And why would we do that?"

"I assume you don't want Andrew Escalante to hang for a murder he did not commit."

"How do you know he did not do it?"

"Because I think I know who did," Clint said, "and I think he's here in Nogales."

"Then if you catch him and bring him back, that will save the boy."

"He's going to need a lawyer," Clint said. "Isobel sent for Freddy and he came, but he says he can't represent Andrew unless you—or Don Alfredo—tell him he can."

"Frederico is not prepared to defend anyone against a murder charge."

"Well, then, I guess that means you'll have to do it."

"I do not practice law in the United States, *Señor* Adams."

"You would," Clint said, "if Don Alfredo told you to, right?"

Ruiz didn't answer.

"Okay," Clint said, "I guess I'll just have to talk to the old man myself, eh? So who's going to take me to see him, you or Freddy?"

THIRTY-ONE

Clint left Frederico and his boss, Manuel Ruiz, to come to that decision. He left the office, registered in the first hotel he came to, then rode Eclipse through Nogales until he found the sheriff's office. He dismounted and walked up to the office door. There was no boardwalk; the buildings in town were flush with the ground. This one was adobe, like the lawyer's office and the hotel, but there were more cracks, some of them significant.

He opened the door and stepped in. There was a man seated at a desk. Actually, he was slumped over it. Clint waited a moment, then heard by the man's breathing that he was asleep.

"Sheriff Lopez?" he asked.

The man didn't stir.

Clint walked to the desk, but didn't touch the man. He'd been shot at more than once by men he had tried to awaken by touching them.

"Sheriff Hector Lopez?" he said, louder.

This time the man lifted his head quickly, looking at Clint with bleary eyes.

"Ah, *señor*," he said, wiping his eyes with his fingers. "I did not hear you come in."

"I'm sorry to interrupt your siesta, Sheriff."

"No, no, it is fine," the sheriff said.

"You are Sheriff Hector Lopez?" Clint asked.

"*Sí, señor*, that is me."

Lopez was about thirty-five, a tall, skinny man with a thin, well-tended mustache that came down along both sides of his mouth. He was wearing a long-sleeved undershirt and jeans, the shirt damp around the neck from perspiration. It wasn't that hot outside, but Clint did notice that it was hotter in the jail for some reason.

"What can I do for you, *señor*?"

"Sheriff Stroby from Nogales told me to talk to you," Clint said.

"Ah, my friend Stroby," Lopez said. "I will be happy to help you in any way I can."

"That's good," Clint said. "I'm looking for a man named Jess Mitchell."

"A gringo?"

"Yes. I believe he's hiding here from a murder charge in the United States."

"Are you a bounty hunter, *señor*?"

"No," Clint said. "My name is Clint Adams. I am also looking for Mitchell because he was using my name."

"Ah," Lopez said, "*El Armero*."

"That's right," Clint said, "the Gunsmith."

"Excuse me, *señor*," Lopez said, standing up. "I am not at my best."

He took a shirt off a hook on the wall and put it on, buttoned it quickly, then tucked it into his pants. The shirt had a badge pinned to it.

"So, this gringo is an accused murderer?"

"Not exactly," Clint said, and then explained the situation to the man.

"*Aiee*," Lopez said, "Don Alfredo's son? You are attempting to prove the boy innocent?"

"Yes, that's part of it," Clint said. "The other part is Mitchell impersonating me. And finally, I'd like to talk with Don Alfredo."

"Oh, I can't help you with that, *señor*," the lawman said. "I do not have the authority to speak with Don Alfredo. For that you would need to speak with his lawyers."

"I have," Clint said. "They're trying to decide now who is going to take me to him. What I need to find out from you is if you have any gringos in town."

"Oh, *sí*, several," Lopez said.

"Did they come in together?"

"No, *señor*, separately," Lopez said. "And I do not think they have spent any time together."

"Where can I find the three of them?"

"Two of them are in the Nogales Hotel," Lopez said. "The third has a room behind the cantina across from the undertaker."

"Do you know their names?"

"Of course," Lopez said. "I am *alguacil*. It is my job."

"Well, as the sheriff, can you tell me their names?" Clint asked.

"*Sí*," Lopez said, "two of them are Smith, and one of them is . . . Jones."

Clint looked disappointed.

"This is not helpful?"

"Not really."

"Ah," Lopez said, "perhaps those are common names for gringos?"

"Yes," Clint said, "very common. I guess I'll just have to go and see each man myself."

"You would require my presence, *señor*?"

"I don't think so, Sheriff," Clint answered. "I just wanted you to know I was in town."

"We are honored to have you."

"Thank you."

Clint started for the door.

"Señor?"

"Yes?"

"Do you intend to kill this gringo, Mitchell, when you find him?"

"I think the choice will be his," Clint said. "I intend to bring him back to Tubac alive."

"But if he resists . . ."

"I'll do what I have to do," Clint said.

"I understand, *señor*."

"But I'll keep you informed."

"I will appreciate that, *Señor* Adams."

"I'm going to take a room in the Nogales," Clint said. "I'll talk to those men first."

"Smith and Jones."

"Yes," Clint said. "I'll find out their real names for you. There might be a reward for them."

"Reward?"

"Who knows?" Clint said.

THIRTY-TWO

Clint went to the Nogales Hotel and registered, got a room on the second floor. At the same time he checked the register to see where the other two gringos were. One was in Room 5, and the other in Room 13. He was in Room 8.

He went to his room first, left his rifle and saddlebags there, then came out and walked to Room 5. He knocked, waited.

The man who answered the door had a gun in his hand. Clint understood. He'd done the same thing countless times. He showed the man his hands.

"No need for that gun," he said.

"Who're you?"

"My name's Clint Adams," he said. "You Smith?"

The man's eyes registered recognition. Other than that, he didn't react.

"I'm Smith."

"What's your real name?"

"Why you wanna know?"

"It wouldn't be Mitchell, would it?" Clint asked. "Jess Mitchell?"

The man didn't answer right away. Clint didn't think it was him anyway. He was too short to match the description Andrew had given him.

"No, my name's not Mitchell," Smith said.

"Okay," Clint said, "thanks."

"That's it?"

"That's it."

Clint started up the hall.

"You don't wanna know who I really am?" the man called.

"No," Clint said. "If you're not Mitchell, I'm not interested in you."

"But—"

Clint turned and walked back to the door. He didn't want them to be yelling back and forth in the hall, potentially warning the man "Jones" in Room 13.

"You're wanted in our country, right?"

"Right."

"Murder?"

"No," the man said. "Just—"

Clint held up a hand.

"Not interested," he said, "but if I was you, I'd get out of here. The sheriff might be taking an interest."

"Okay," the man said. "Thanks."

As the door closed, Clint walked up the hall to Room 13. He knocked, and then "Jones" answered the door with his gun in his hand.

"Yeah?"

The man had hair as red as a carrot.

"Sorry," Clint said. "Wrong room."

He walked down the hall.

In the lobby of the hotel he ran into Frederico Rodriguez.

"Looking for me, Freddy?" he asked.

"Yes," Frederico said, "we have decided that *Señor* Ruiz will take you to see Don Alfredo."

"When?"

"Now," Frederico said. "Right now."

Clint frowned. He still had the third man to see, the other "Smith."

"Ready?" Frederico asked.

"Yes, okay," Clint said. He could check the third man out when he got back. If he went after him now, he didn't know when he'd get another chance to talk to Don Alfredo.

"Let's go," he said.

THIRTY-THREE

Don Alfredo Escalante's ranchero was about ten miles out of town. Manual Ruiz, much too old to sit a horse, rode out in a buggy. Frederico was left behind in the office to do some work.

"I must warn you . . ." Ruiz said as they rode out together.

"About what?" Clint was riding alongside the buggy.

"Don Alfredo does not like surprises."

"Meaning you didn't send word ahead to let him know we were coming, right?"

"Yes."

"So you're thinking he won't agree to talk to me."

Ruiz didn't reply.

"Well," Clint said. "I think he will."

"What makes you say that?"

"People seem to like to talk to me," Clint said.

"Because of who you are?"

"That could be it," Clint said. "Normally, I don't like to

take advantage of that, but in this instance I think I'll make an exception."

When they arrived, several ranch hands—vaqueros—stepped forward to grab Ruiz's horse and assist him down from his buggy seat. They obviously knew who he was, and knew how they were supposed to treat him when he appeared.

Once Ruiz was on the ground, the hands all turned and looked at Clint. Ruiz said something to them in Spanish, and one of them stepped forward and held out his hand.

"You can give him your horse," Ruiz said.

"If he's not careful, he'll lose a finger or two," Clint said.

"He knows," Ruiz said.

Clint shrugged, dismounted, and handed Eclipse's reins to the man.

"We can go inside," Ruiz said. "They will see to the horses."

The old man approached the large house with a halting gait, and then a vaquero appeared at his elbow to help him up the steps.

"*Gracias*," he said when they'd reached the top.

The front door opened and a Mexican wearing a white jacket appeared. He said something to Ruiz.

"Speak English, Carlos," Ruiz said. "Mr. Adams does not speak Spanish."

"I will tell Don Alfredo you are here," Carlos said. "Please wait inside."

They entered the house, stopped just inside the door while Carlos closed and locked it. The floor was made of many pieces of slate. The house itself was made of a combination of wood and adobe.

"This is Mr. Clint Adams," Ruiz said, "also known as the Gunsmith. He came to speak with Don Alfredo."

"I will tell him, *Señor* Ruiz."

Carlos, who looked to be in his sixties, moved away quietly, his footsteps making no sound at all.

"You didn't tell him why I wanted to speak to him," Clint pointed out.

"If I did," Ruiz said, "he probably would not speak to you."

"And now?"

"He might be polite because you are here already."

They waited in silence the rest of the time and Carlos finally reappeared.

"Don Alfredo will see you," he said.

"*Muy bien,*" Ruiz said, and started to move forward.

"No, not you, *señor,*" Carlos said, "just *Señor* Adams."

Ruiz took the news in stride.

"Go ahead, *señor,*" he said. "I wish you luck."

Clint followed Carlos.

THIRTY-FOUR

Carlos led Clint to a room in back of the house that was furnished in the plush style of many whorehouses he had been in. It surprised him that Don Alfredo Escalante was sitting in the center of it on a red sofa.

"You are surprised," Escalante said. "You expected cruci-fixes, statues, and old-fashioned furniture?"

"Actually," Clint said, "I wasn't expecting much of any-thing, but yes, I am surprised."

"Sit down, please. Would you like something to drink? Or perhaps some coffee?"

"Strong and black," Clint said.

"Carlos?"

"Sí, jefe."

Clint took a seat in a rich-looking armchair.

"You were expecting me."

"Sí."

"How?"

"I have ways of getting information," he said, "especially when it comes to my children."

"So you know Andrew is in jail?"

"Yes."

"And what for?"

"Yes."

Clint studied the man. Whereas Ruiz looked eighty, Escalante may have been eighty but could have passed for sixty. He was extremely fit, wearing white pants and a white shirt with an open collar.

"And you intend to do nothing?"

"I intend," Escalante said, "to have coffee with my guest."

"What about Ruiz?"

"What about him?"

"He's still standing in your front hall," Clint said. "I think he needs to sit down."

"Manuel is being cared for," Escalante said.

Carlos appeared with a silver tray, bearing a silver coffeepot and china cups. He set it all down, filled the cups, and withdrew.

Escalante picked up one of the cups and sipped it.

"I thought you would take it with milk," Clint said.

"I have never acquired a taste for *café con leche*," the man said. "I prefer my *café* to be *negro*."

Clint picked up the coffee cup. It smelled wonderful, tasted even better.

"*Bien?*" Escalante asked.

"It's very good. Thank you." He put the cup down. "So you have people watching your children for you?"

"Not specifically," the older man said in unaccented English, "but I receive reports."

"Then you know that Isobel shot me when she thought I was the reason her brother was in jail."

"Yes," he said. "And I appreciate the fact that you did not shoot her, or have her arrested."

"She needed help, she didn't need to be arrested," Clint said.

"And you are helping her."

"You're the one who should be helping her," Clint said. "And Andrew."

"My children made the decision to go out on their own," he said. "They took what I offered them and threw it back in my face."

"I think perhaps you overreacted to their desire to be their own people."

"I built all this," he said, waving his arms, "for them. How do you think I felt when they said they did not want it?"

"I understand—"

"Do you?" Escalante asked. "Do you have children of your own?"

"No."

"Then you cannot understand, can you?"

"No, I suppose not."

"No."

Clint picked up his cup and drank again. Escalante seemed to be annoyed enough to kick him out at that point.

"Do you know why I agreed to see you?"

"No."

"I am aware of your reputation, and I wanted to hear what you had to say. So go ahead, please. Convince me to change my mind."

"I'm not sure I can, now that I'm here," Clint said. "I didn't realize how hurt you were. I didn't realize how much petulance had to do with your decision to do nothing to help your children."

Don Alfredo Escalante stared at Clint for several moments, and then abruptly started laughing.

"That was very good," he said. "Petulance. Insult me by comparing me to a petulant child. Very good. Hoping that would force me to act to show you that I am not what you accuse me of."

"It was worth a try," Clint said. "Look, I'm trying to help your children. I'm looking for a man named Jess Mitchell. I think he's in Nogales. I'll find out for sure tonight, when I get back to town. If it's him, I'll be taking him back to Tubac."

"And how will you prove that he is the killer, and not my son?"

"I don't know," Clint said. "Maybe I'll be able to get him to admit it."

"And maybe you'll have to kill him before that happens," Escalante said. "Then what?"

"Then Andrew will need a good lawyer. And good lawyers cost money. Unless you send yours."

"My lawyers do not practice law in the United States."

"Then you can hire an American lawyer," Clint said.

"And why should I?"

"Are we back to that again?" Clint asked. "They're your children."

"Tell Isobel to come back."

"What?"

"Tell her to come back and ask me for help."

"And then you'll help?"

"I do not know. But we'll see."

Clint stood up.

"Are we finished?"

"I am," Clint said. "I've got work to do."

"Don't you want to talk to my wife?" Escalante asked. "See if she can have an influence over me?"

"Nobody can influence you," Clint said. "You are definitely your own man, something you can't seem to appreciate in your own son."

"My son? His own man?"

"If you can't see that, then you need help," Clint said.

"*Señor*," Escalante said, "you have no idea—"

"You're right, I don't," Clint said. "At least, I didn't when I got here, but I have a better idea now. Thanks for seeing me, Don Alfredo. And thanks for the coffee."

"*Señor*—"

"I'm sure you'll know everything that happens right after it happens," Clint said.

He walked out, found his way back to where Manuel Ruiz was seated—still in the hall. Someone had brought the old man a straight-backed wooden chair. He looked extremely uncomfortable.

"Is that all?" Ruiz asked. "That did not take very long."

"No, it didn't," Clint said.

"Did you accomplish anything?"

"I doubt it."

"Señor?"

Clint turned, saw Carlos standing there.

"Yes?"

"Doña Estrella would like to speak with you before you leave."

"Is that a fact?"

"Sí, señor."

Clint looked at Ruiz.

"You had better go," he said, shifting a bit in the chair.

"Get Carlos to bring you some coffee," Clint said. "It's really good."

He turned to the servant and said, "All right, lead the way."

THIRTY-FIVE

Clint followed Carlos to the kitchen, which surprised him. It also surprised him to find a handsome woman in her fifties there, kneading some dough. She was using her fists on it, and he wondered whose face she was envisioning there.

"*Señora*, Clint Adams," Carlos said.

"*Gracias*, Carlos," she said. "That is all."

As Carlos left, Estrella Escalante looked at Clint, wiping her hands off on the apron she wore, which covered her from the neck down.

"Thank you for agreeing to see me, *Señor* Adams," she said.

"That's all right, *señora*."

"You have finished talking to my husband, I assume?" she asked.

"Yes."

"And are you frustrated?"

"Very much so."

"Then you know how I feel every day since the children left home," she said. "I was hoping that someone like you would be able to talk sense into him."

Her English was not as good as her husband's, but it was only slightly accented. Clint could see past the lines in her face and neck to the beauty she had once been.

"I'm afraid I wasn't able to talk any sense into him," he said, holding his hat in his hand.

"Have you been able to help my stepson at all?" she asked.

He explained to her everything he had done so far, and what he intended to do. He even told her how Isobel had shot him.

"I am very sorry about what my stepdaughter did to you," she said, "but I am grateful for all you have tried to do to help Andrew and Isobel. I love them like my own children."

"If I find Jess Mitchell and take him back to Tubac," he said, "we might be able to get Andrew out of jail."

"But how would you prove that this man, Mitchell, is the real killer?"

"As I told your husband, maybe I can get him to confess."

"But that is only if he does not force you to kill him."

"Well . . . yes."

"And if he knows he is going back to the United States to face a murder charge, that would be likely, eh?"

"I'm going to do my best to get him back there alive, *señora*."

"I believe you are, *señor*," she said. "I can tell by your actions so far that you are an honorable man."

"Thank you, *señora.*"

He turned to leave. She moved so quickly she was beside him before he knew it, her hand on his arm.

"*Señor*, I have some money that my husband does not know about," she said. "It should be enough to hire a lawyer. Please let me know if you need it."

"I will, *señora*," Clint said, "but I'm hoping to resolve this without the need of a lawyer."

"I hope you can, *señor*," she said, "and I thank you with all my heart."

He nodded. She removed her hand from his arm and he left the kitchen.

Ruiz was still sitting in the hard chair when Clint got back to the hall. The old man was shifting uncomfortably but abruptly stopped when Clint appeared.

"Are we finished?" he asked, looking up at Clint hopefully.

"He doesn't want to talk to you before we leave?" Clint asked.

"I am sure he has nothing to say to me, *señor*," Ruiz said.

"Are you going to get into trouble for bringing me here?"

"I have been in trouble with Don Alfredo before," the man said with a shrug.

Clint put his hand out to help the older man to his feet, then offered his elbow to help him down the front stairs. Once they were outside, the vaqueros brought Eclipse and the buggy around, and helped Ruiz up into his seat. Clint was secretly satisfied to see one vaquero hiding his bleeding hand. Eclipse had taken at least a piece out of the man, if not a finger.

Ruiz turned the buggy around and looked at Clint.

"Did you find satisfaction, *señor*?"

"Very little, I'm afraid," Clint said, "but the *señora* seems to be a remarkable woman."

"You have no idea, *señor*," Ruiz said, and snapped the reins at his horse.

THIRTY-SIX

Back in town, Clint helped Ruiz get his rig back to the livery, and then accompanied the old man back to his office.

"Thank you," Ruiz said at the door.

"*Señor* Ruiz, I was told Don Alfredo has several lawyers."

"*Sí*, that is true," the older man said. "He has me, and Frederico works for me. He uses one other lawyer for his business matters."

"So no one who specializes in criminal matters?" Clint asked.

"No," Ruiz said. "Don Alfredo is not a criminal."

"Okay, well, thank you for taking me to see him."

"What will you do now?"

"See if I can find Mitchell and squeeze a confession out of him."

"I wish you luck."

Ruiz went into his building and Clint walked to his hotel.

* * *

It was late afternoon, still time to find the third gringo, the other "Smith," and see if he was Jess Mitchell. If he wasn't, then Clint would have to admit that he might have gone the wrong way, the wrong direction. If Mitchell had fled north—or east or west—then he was gone. Getting Andrew Escalante out of jail would be almost impossible. They needed that confession.

If he wanted to, he could continue to track Mitchell when he got back to the United States, to make sure the man did not ever impersonate him again. But that wouldn't help Andrew. He'd go to trial, and probably be hanged. Clint couldn't let that happen, especially now that he had two women—Isobel and Estrella—depending on him.

He left his hotel and walked to the cantina the sheriff had told him about, which had rooms to rent behind it. It was an adobe building, all on one level.

He entered and approached the bar, wanting simply to be another customer for a little while. The place was busy, all the tables taken, three women with long black hair and peasant blouses working the floor. Behind the bar was an evil-looking man in his thirties. He had black hair, a black mustache and beard, and a shirt with the sleeves pushed up over large forearms. He looked as if his face would crack if he ever tried to smile. The bar top was pitted and filthy.

"Whiskey," Clint said. He figured drinking something from a bottle was the safest course of action.

The bartender poured him a shot glass of whiskey and took his money.

Looking at the bartender, Clint decided the man would not react well to questions. Not direct questions anyway.

He drank his whiskey, checking the room. He did not see any other gringos in the room but himself. Every table was taken up by two or three Mexican men, but nobody seemed to be paying any special attention to him.

The women kept working the room. They looked enough alike to be in the same family, but he noticed they were of varying ages. And while two were tall and slender, the older woman had a lusher figure packed onto about five inches less height.

He turned back to the bar and asked for another whiskey. The bartender poured it without a word. Clint wondered if the man spoke much English.

He decided to find out.

"Do you speak English?" he asked.

The man glared at him, then nodded.

"I heard you had rooms to rent in the back," Clint said. "I'm looking."

"No room," the man said.

"Oh? Why not?"

"All taken."

"I see. Okay, well, thanks."

He finished his whiskey and decided to leave. The room didn't feel right to him. If he started to ask questions, people would begin to notice him.

He decided to find out what he needed to know on the outside. Only it would have to wait until after dark. He didn't want to be seen peering in the windows.

He left the cantina, and while he didn't notice anyone specific watching him when he entered, he felt there were more than one set of eyes on him as he left.

* * *

Mitchell opened the door to the light knock, saw Rosa standing in the hall.

"Not ready for you, honey," he said.

"There was a man in the cantina," she said. "A gringo."

"What'd he want?"

"A room," she said. "He asked José about a room."

"What did José tell him?"

"No rooms."

"Okay," he said, "okay. Come and tell me if he comes back in, okay?"

"I will."

"And come back in a couple of hours anyway." He hooked his finger in the front of her blouse, so that the finger was between her breasts.

"*Sí*," she said, "I will be back."

She went down the hall, and he watched her walk until she was gone.

Rosa didn't like the gringo. She thought she was his favorite, however, because she squealed a lot when she was in bed with him. He seemed to like that.

All the girls, and José, knew that he was on the run from someone. When they saw the gringo walk in, and then leave after two drinks, José sent her back to warn Mitchell. After all, he had agreed to pay José a lot for the room, and the service.

Rosa wouldn't have minded if Mitchell left them this week. She was ready for him to go.

And she wouldn't have minded if the new gringo came in and stayed awhile.

THIRTY-SEVEN

Clint didn't know anyone in Nogales except the two lawyers, Ruiz and Frederico. He had to kill time until dark, but he didn't want to do it with them, so he found a small cantina—smaller than the one he'd just come from—and had something to eat alone.

However, while he was sitting there, Frederico came in, and Clint didn't think it was a coincidence. The young lawyer stopped just inside the door, looked around, and when he spotted Clint, came walking over.

"I have been looking for you," he said, standing awkwardly.

"Have you eaten?"

"No."

"Sit. Order something."

A waiter came over and Frederico simply ordered what Clint was having—burritos, rice and beans, and beer—*cerveza*—to go with it.

"What can I do for you, Freddy?" Clint asked.

"I wanted to know what happened with Don Alfredo," the young lawyer said.

"Didn't *Señor* Ruiz tell you?"

"He told me nothing," Frederico said.

"Because you're a junior partner?"

"I am not a partner at all," he said. "He treats me like a clerk."

"Sorry to hear it," Clint said, "but you are a lawyer, right?"

"*Sí*, I am a lawyer—a lawyer who is not allowed to practice law. But that is not what I want to talk about. Did you talk with Don Alfredo?"

"I did," Clint said, "and to *Señora* Escalante."

"He allowed that?" Frederico's surprise was evident.

"He knew nothing about it," Clint said. "She called me in when I was about to leave."

"Is she—what did she say?"

"She wants me to help Andrew and Isobel," Clint said, "and she offered to do whatever she could do to help."

"And what did he say?"

"He didn't offer to help."

"He will do nothing?"

"Apparently not."

"And what are you doing?"

"I've got one more man to check out," Clint said. "If he's Mitchell, I'll take him back to Tubac with me."

"But Andrew will still need a lawyer?"

"Yes."

"All right," Frederico said. "When you go back, I want to go with you."

"What for?"

"I want to help. I will represent Andrew."

"Does *Señor* Ruiz know?"

"No," Frederico said. "I will not tell him until I come back."

"Are you doing this for Isobel?"

"Yes."

Clint shrugged. It really didn't matter to him why the man was doing it.

The waiter came with Frederico's plate and set it down before him.

"Well, eat your food," Clint said. "When we're done, I'll go over and check on my man. If it's him, we'll be leaving in the morning."

"I will be ready."

According to what Escalante and Ruiz had said, Frederico wouldn't be able to practice law in the United States, but Clint decided not to point that out at the moment.

THIRTY-EIGHT

It was dark when Clint got back to the cantina. He entered the alley next to it, saw several windows there lit up. They must have had a few rooms back there. Maybe even on the other side of the building, too. He was going to have to peer in a few windows.

And when he did, would he know he was looking at Jess Mitchell? Hopefully, the man was the only gringo in the place.

He got to the first window and looked in, saw a Mexican man sitting on a bed, inspecting a big hole in one of his socks while he was still wearing it. He was really involved, and there was nobody else in the room with him.

He moved on to the next window, saw another Mexican man sitting on the bed, picking at something between the toes of his right foot. Again, alone in the room.

He moved on.

He looked into the third window, saw one of the black-haired girls from the cantina talking to someone who was out of sight.

And then she took off her blouse.

When the knock came at the door, Mitchell answered it, figuring it was Rosa coming back. He was right. He put his gun down and let her in.

"Did that gringo come back?" he asked.

"No."

"Did he ever ask about me?"

"No."

"What did he do?"

"He had two drinks and then he left."

He walked to the far end of the room, gave it some thought, then decided it was a coincidence. Gringos came into the cantina every once in a while. After all, this was Nogales, right near the border. Plus, there was no way anyone from Tubac could know he was here.

"Okay," he said, turning to face her, "take off your clothes."

Clint watched the girl remove her blouse, revealing the sweetest little breasts, topped with very brown, hard nipples. Next, she slid her skirt down to the floor and stepped out of it. No underthings. A big black bush between her slender legs. She then turned slowly, showing Clint and whoever was in the room a smooth, round little butt.

When she had turned completely around again, she stopped, and the man in the room came into view. Clint couldn't see his face, though, and it didn't help when he fell to his knees and buried her face in her black bush. All he could see was that the man did not have black hair, and was dressed better than most of the Mexicans he'd seen since he got to Nogales.

He watched as the man buried his face and kept it there so long Clint thought he might be suffocating. It was only the woman's reactions that told him the man was still conscious.

Finally, the man withdrew his head, stood up, lifted the woman in his arms, then turned and walked to the bed. As he set her down, Clint saw his face. A gringo. The other Mr. Smith.

And with any luck, Jess Mitchell.

Mitchell dropped Rosa onto the bed, then quickly removed his own clothes. His hard cock sprang free and Rosa fell on it, taking it into her mouth hungrily.

Mitchell moved his hips while she sucked it, fucking her mouth. She did this part really well; it was the squealing she did when he was inside her that he didn't like.

So he put his hands on her head and figured he'd just let her do this for a while . . .

Clint moved away from the door, so he never saw the man take off his clothes. He moved down the rest of the alley, ignoring the two remaining windows, which were dark. When he got to the back, he was satisfied to discover the place had a back door. In addition, it wasn't a very sturdy one. He pressed his shoulder to it and the door popped open.

He found himself in a dimly lit hallway. There were no gas lamps, just a couple of oil lamps on the wall. Clint figured this was the hallway that led to the rooms. At the far end was a curtained doorway that probably led to the cantina.

There were five doors on each side of the hall. The room he'd been looking into was the middle one on the left side.

He drew his gun and started down the hall.

THIRTY-NINE

He stopped at the door to listen. He could hear noise coming from the cantina. He pressed his ear to the door, heard some grunting and groaning that sounded familiar.

He tried the doorknob, found it locked. If he had to kick in the door, it might make too much noise. Even if it wasn't heard in the cantina, it might be heard by someone in the other rooms.

He decided to try something straightforward.

He knocked.

When Mitchell heard the knock, he turned and looked at the door.

"Well," he said, "somebody finally decided to take us up on our offer."

He had asked two of the girls to be with him at one time. So far, they had refused. Maybe one of them had finally decided to try it. It was probably Helena. Up to now, she'd tried everything but that.

"Let her in, honey," he said, pulling his dick out of Rosa's mouth.

She got off the bed and reached for her blouse.

"No, no," he said, "just go to the door naked. She won't mind."

Rosa turned and trotted to the door.

When the naked girl opened the door, Clint pointed his gun at her and held his finger to his lips. She stood still, recognizing him from when he'd come into the cantina. Instead of showing fear, she reached up and caressed one of her small breasts. He smiled at her, briefly caressed the other one—small, but firm—then motioned her to step back.

"Well?" Mitchell asked. "Who is it? Helena? Or—"

"On your feet, Mitchell!" Clint said.

The naked man on the bed leaped to his feet, made a move toward his gun.

"You won't make it," Clint said.

The man looked at him.

"Who are you?" he asked.

"Clint Adams."

The man considered this, then pulled his hand away from his gun.

"Against anyone else, I'd try it," he said.

"Smart man," Clint said. "You are Jess Mitchell, aren't you?"

"What's it to you?"

Clint looked at the girl.

"You can get dressed," he said. "He won't be needing you tonight."

"And you?" she asked. "Will you need me?" She reached up with both hands, rubbed her nipples.

"Unfortunately," Clint said, "no."

She pouted, and picked up her clothes.

"Close the door on your way out," Clint said.

She nodded, got dressed, and then went out into the hall.

"You shouldn't have let her go," the man said.

"Why not?"

"I'm a paying customer," he said. "They're not gonna let me go that easy."

Clint realized he was right. The girl would undoubtedly run to the bartender and tell him what was happening.

"Get dressed, Mitchell."

"I don't think so," the naked man said.

"Either get dressed or I'll drag you out and put you on a horse naked—all the way back to Tubac."

"I'll get dressed."

FORTY

They went out the back door, Clint holding his own gun and carrying Mitchell's tucked into his belt. Despite the fact that the man had not yet admitted to being Jess Mitchell, Clint felt he had the right man.

"Where to now?" Mitchell asked.

"The livery stable," Clint said. "I assume you have a horse there."

When the man didn't reply, Clint jabbed him in the kidney with his gun barrel.

"Yes!" Mitchell blurted out.

"Then let's go."

They made their way in the darkness to the livery. The streets were pretty much deserted, noise coming from the various saloons along the way.

When they reached the livery, they found the front doors open.

"Inside," Clint said.

"I left my saddlebags behind," Mitchell complained.

"So did I," Clint said. "It's not important. We're getting out of town now."

Clint didn't feel he had the time to go back to his hotel room. He also didn't have the time to let Frederico know he was leaving town.

"They're gonna come after us, you know."

"I doubt it," Clint said. "I doubt they've become that fond of you."

Mitchell laughed. "You don't understand," he said. "When I said I was a paying customer, what I meant was, I owe them money. A lot of money. They'll come after us, all right."

"Then we better get moving," Clint said, holstering his gun. "Saddle your horse. And don't try anything while I'm saddling mine."

Rosa went directly to the bartender, José, and told him what happened.

"Who was the gringo?" José asked.

"The same man who came in earlier today," she told him. "He . . . touched me."

"That's not a crime," José said, looking a her. "But running out on the bill is."

"Smith is not running out," she said. "I think the other man is taking him away."

"Not if I have anything to say about it," José said, glowering. "Find Eusabio and the others."

When they were both saddled, they rode out. Normally, Clint would have ridden through town to ride north to the border.

"We'll ride out this way and circle around town," Clint said. "Just to be on the safe side."

"Whatever you say, Adams," Mitchell said. "You're in charge—for now."

José, Eusabio, and three other men went down the hall to Mitchell's room, and found it empty.

"His saddlebags are still here," Eusabio said. "And his rifle."

"He was taken against his will," one of the other men said.

"Perhaps," Jose said. "Is there money in the saddle-bags?"

Eusabio checked.

"No, he must have his money with him."

"If the other gringo took him at gunpoint, they're probably heading for the border."

"Are we goin' after them?" Eusabio asked.

"Oh yes," Jose said. "That gringo owe me money—a lot of money. Everyone saddle up."

FORTY-ONE

"We ain't gonna camp for the night?" Mitchell asked after they had left Nogales behind.

"No," Clint said. "We'll keep going until we reach Nogales on the American side."

"You're crazy," the man said. "We'll break our necks out here."

"It's not that far," Clint said. "You just want me to camp so your friends can catch up to us."

"Oh, they ain't my friends," the man said. "They think I ran out on my bill. They'll kill you and me, and take our money."

"All the more reason to keep going, right?" Clint asked.

"I suppose so."

"So," Clint said, "you ready to admit you're Jess Mitchell?"

"You ready to prove I am?" the other man asked.

"Guess I can't," Clint said. "We left your saddlebags behind."

"Yeah, too bad."

"Unless . . ."

"Unless what?"

"I can get the sheriff of Mexican Nogales to send the saddlebags to the sheriff on the American side," Clint said. "There must be something in there with your name on it."

"Don't count on it."

But the man didn't sound very confident.

They rode into Nogales on the American side in a couple of hours. The streets were as empty as they had been on the other side of the border, and similarly, they could hear some noise from the saloons.

"Can we get a drink?" the prisoner asked.

"No," Clint said. "We're going to the sheriff's office."

"He probably won't be there," the man sad. "We got a better chance of getting a drink."

"I'm going to stick you in a cell, and then go get myself a cold beer."

"You're a hard man."

"Tell me your name and we'll go get a beer," Clint said.

"That's even harder," the man said. "I guess you better just toss my ass into a cell. But you better get ready for José and his amigos 'cause they'll be here soon."

"You think they'd follow us over the border?"

"Oh, yeah."

"But . . . why?"

"Well," he said, "I told you I owed them a lot of money, right?"

"Right."

"What I didn't tell you is that I don't have any money,"

he said. "They'll kill me when they find out. And you, if you get between me and them."

"How did you think you were going to get out of there without paying?"

"I had some money owed to me that was going to be sent to the bank in Nogales."

"When?"

"It was supposed to have arrived days ago."

"So somebody didn't pay you for a job."

The man shrugged.

"And that job was killing Joe Widmar?"

Still didn't answer.

"So somebody in Tubac paid you to kill Joe Widmar," Clint said. "Why?"

"Let's get me to a cell," the prisoner said. "I'll be safer there when José and his men come in."

"For once I agree with you," Clint said.

FORTY-TWO

Sheriff Stroby was in his office late, going through wanted posters, when the door opened. Clint walked in, pushing the man he believed to be Jess Mitchell ahead of him.

"This Mitchell?" he asked.

"I hope so," Clint said. "If he's not, I wasted a lot of time. Got a cell for him?"

"Nice and clean."

"And some food?" the prisoner asked.

"We'll see," Stroby said. He grabbed the key off the wall peg. "Come on."

Clint waited where he was, listening to the sound of the cell closing, until the sheriff reappeared.

"Coffee?" Stroby asked.

"Sure."

Stroby poured two mugs, handed one to Clint, then sat behind his desk. He dropped the key on the desk.

"Nothin' on him to identify him?" Stroby asked.

"No," Clint said. "I had to grab him and get out after dark, then come straight here."

"Now what?" the lawman asked. "Back to Tubac?"

"That's the plan, but there may be a problem."

"Like what?"

Clint explained about the bill the prisoner had run up at the cantina across the border.

"That doesn't sound so hard," Stroby said.

"They'll be here soon," Clint said, "probably right behind us, so if you've got a solution, I'd like to hear it."

"Simple. Pay them what he owes them," Stroby said. "How much is it?"

"I didn't ask him."

"Maybe it's enough to kill him for," Stroby said, "but enough for you to handle."

"Me?"

"Well, who else is gonna pay 'em?"

"He says somebody from Tubac owes him money, was supposed to wire it to him."

"You know who that is? So you can get it back from them?"

"No."

"Well," Stroby said, "it's up to you. You wanna trade lead over him, I'll back you."

"Why would you do that?"

"Because he's in my jail," Stroby said. "Nobody takes anybody out of my jail."

"You got a deputy?"

"Nope."

"Anybody you can deputize?"

"Not tonight."

"Okay, then," Clint said. "Instead of dragging you into this, maybe we should just get back on the road and head for Tubac tonight."

"I know you have a great horse," Stroby said, "but you can't count on his horse being as surefooted as yours. If it steps in a chuckhole and breaks a leg, you'll be stuck out there with one of you on foot. Even if you ride double, they'll catch up to you. I think my idea's better. Stay here. When they show up, we'll find out how much he owes them. A few dollars might clear all this up."

"I think it's going to be more than a few dollars," Clint said, "but if you're willing to back me . . ."

"It's my job to back you," Stroby said. "Let's get some food in here and we can all eat and wait for them to show up."

"Well, okay, then," Clint said. "Just tell me where to go to get the food."

José Baca said to his men, "Nobody runs out on me, owing me money. That gringo is going to be sorry he ever came to Nogales."

The other four men sat their horses behind him, and nodded.

"What about the other *Americano*, José?" Eusabio asked. "Rosa said he took the gringo by force."

"Then he put his nose in my business," Jose said. "He will pay as well."

They were just outside Nogales on the American side of the border. The four men were waiting for their boss's order to go in.

"And what of the law?" one of the other men asked.

"That is Stroby," José said. "He is alone."

"He is a good lawman," Eusabio said. "He will not stand by and watch."

"That is fine with me," José said. "We have a past, he and I. Perhaps we can put that to rest tonight as well."

"So we are going in?" Eusabio asked.

José looked back at his men. They were all experienced pistoleros.

"*Sí*," he said, "we go in."

FORTY-THREE

Clint brought some steak dinners back to the sheriff's office from a nearby cantina. He went into the cell block and gave one to Mitchell, along with coffee.

"What, no beer?"

"Just bad jailhouse coffee," Clint said. "Want it or not?"

"I'll take it," Mitchell said. "Thanks."

"You're welcome, Mitchell."

Mitchell smiled at Clint's attempt to get him to react to his name. He took his meal back to his cot, set the cup of coffee on the floor, and started sawing on his meat with a mostly dull knife.

Clint went back into the office and sat across from the sheriff, both using his desk as a table.

"You know a bartender named José something, runs a cantina across the border in Nogales?"

Stroby nodded.

"That's José Baca," he said. "Yeah, I know him. He used to run a business here, too, until I ran him out of town."

"Has he been back since?"

"No," said Stroby. "I can see him using this to kill two birds with one stone."

"With you being one of the birds?"

Stroby nodded.

"He'd kill a lawman?" Clint asked.

Stroby nodded and said, "Why not? He can slip right back across the border. Nobody can touch him unless he comes back."

"I tell you what," Clint said. "If he kills you, I'll go across the border and get him."

"That makes me feel a lot better about this whole thing," Stroby said.

They finished the remainder of their meal in silence.

About twenty minutes later they heard horses. Stroby went to the front window and looked out.

"Looks like them," he said. "Lead rider looks like José."

"Guess we should go out and confront them."

"Wait . . ." Stroby said. "Yeah, they're reining in their horses in front of the jail."

"How many?" Clint asked.

"He's got four men with him, that I can see."

Clint got out of his chair, but Stroby held a hand out to him.

"Let me go out and talk to him first," the lawman suggested.

"Alone? What if they just gun you down?"

"I said Baca would kill a lawman, but not without provocation. He's not just gonna gun me down until we've at least talked. Just cover me from the window."

"Okay."

Stroby took a shotgun from the gun rack, went to the door, and stepped out. Clint decided to crack the door and cover him from there. That way he wouldn't have to take the time to break the glass on the window, or take a chance on firing through the glass.

When Stroby stepped out, he clearly saw José Baca in the light from a nearby lamp. The sheriff stood relaxed, just holding the shotgun across his body.

"José," he said. "What brings you and your boys to this side of the border?"

"From the looks of those horses," Baca said, indicating Eclipse and the horse Mitchell had ridden in on, "you have the two men I'm looking for, Sheriff."

"I have one man in a cell," Stroby admitted. "You lookin' for him?"

"Sí," Baca said, "I have some business with him."

"If you have business with him, you must know his name."

"Smith."

Stroby laughed.

"Lots of Smiths in this country, José," Stroby said. "How much money does he owe you?"

"I do not know exactly," Baca admitted, "but he has eaten much of my food, and used three of my whores many times. And, of course, his room."

"Sounds like a lot of money," Stroby said, "but I'm not sure I have your man."

"I will come in and look at him," Baca said.

"And if he is the man you want?"

"If he pays me, I will take my men and go away."

"And if he can't pay you?"

Baca's face darkened. "That would not be a good thing, Sheriff."

"I tell you what, José," Stroby said. "I suddenly remember runnin' you out of town and tellin' you not to come back. So I think you and your men better be on your way."

"You will not let me in?"

"No," Stroby said. "Be on your way."

Baca firmed his jaw and said, "I cannot do that, Sheriff."

"Then we have a problem, José."

"*Sí*, we do."

Stroby could see that Baca was aware he was under a gun from the jailhouse.

"I will give you ten minutes to give the man to me, Sheriff," he said.

"And then what?"

"Then we will come in and get him."

"That wouldn't be a good idea, José."

"Then give him to me, and you and the other gringo can live. You are outnumbered."

"That other gringo is Clint Adams, José," Stroby said. "You heard of him?"

He could see by the look on the man's face that he had.

"So I think my odds are pretty good. You givin' me ten minutes? I'll give you nine, then I'm comin' back out."

Stroby backed up. Clint opened the door for him and the lawman stepped through. Clint closed the door.

"Hope you don't mind me mentioning you," Stroby said.

"No, but I got an idea while you were out there."

"Is it a good one?"

"I think it may be—for me."

FORTY-FOUR

Stroby brought Mitchell out of his cell and into his office.

"What's goin' on?" he demanded.

"José's out there with four men," Stroby said. "We're outnumbered. I'm afraid I've got to hand you over to them."

"You can't do that," the prisoner said. "They'll kill me." He looked at Clint. "You said you were takin' me back to Tubac."

"Well, that won't do me any good unless you're actually Jess Mitchell."

"Hey, wait a min—"

"I don't care what his name is," Stroby said. "I'm handin' him over. He's probably nobody. And I ain't getting killed for nobody."

"If he can get Andrew Escalante out of jail, his old man's going to be very appreciative, Sheriff," Clint said. "And I mean to you."

"And what about me?" the prisoner asked.

"What about you?"

"Will his father be appreciative to me?"

"I guess so, but only if you're—"

"Okay," the man said, "okay, I'm Jess Mitchell. Ya happy now?"

"And you were the one impersonating me in Tubac?" Clint asked.

"That's right."

"And you killed Joe Widmar?"

"I ain't admittin' to that."

"What about Andrew Escalante? Did he kill him?"

Mitchell hesitated, then said, "No."

"If he's not admitting he did it, what good is he?" Stroby asked.

"I can tell you who paid to have him killed."

"Why would someone do that?"

"For his property. They found important minerals in the ground, and he wouldn't sell."

"So who hired it done?"

"It was the mayor."

"And you'll testify to that?"

"Yeah, yeah," Mitchell said, "now what do we do about them?" He jerked his chin toward the street.

"Don't worry," Clint said. "We'll take care of them. Meanwhile, back in your cell."

"Hey—"

"You'll be safe in there."

Stroby locked him up and came back out.

"I guess he doesn't realize that if he gives the mayor up, the mayor will give him up. They'll both be arrested for murder."

"And Andrew will go free."

"All that's left is to take care of José and his men."

"You want a shotgun?" Stroby asked.

"No, I'm good."

"Eight minutes," Stroby said, looking at his watch.

"Why make them wait?" Clint asked.

They turned and went to the door.

José and Stroby had spoken in English, so the rest of the men hadn't understood. But they did understand the words "Clint Adams" and "Gunsmith."

"Did he say something about the Gunsmith?" Eusabio asked.

"Yes," Baca said, "he is on his way. The quicker we finish here, the better."

At that point, the door to the sheriff's office opened and two men stepped out. The sheriff was holding his shotgun with more intent.

As Clint and Stroby stepped out, the five men turned their attention to them.

"You wanna do this on horseback?" Stroby asked Baca.

"This does not have to be done, Sheriff," Baca said.

"Did you tell them who this man is?" the lawman asked, pointing to Baca's men and then to Clint.

"It does not matter," Baca said. "They will obey me."

"Then tell them to get ready to die," Clint said.

Baca had one split second of doubt, but he was committed. Clint could see it in his eyes.

The other four kept their eyes on Baca, which gave Clint and Stroby a clear advantage but only if they moved first.

They did.

Watch for

FORT REVENGE

358th novel in the exciting GUNSMITH series
from Jove

Coming in October!